I DON'T
WANT TO BE YOUR
SHADOW

Deborah Aydt

SCHOLASTIC BOOK SERVICES
New York Toronto London Auckland Sydney Tokyo

For Raymond F. DeVantier Jr.,
Elaine Pinkerton and
Robert and Mary Lou Mayhew ...
thoughtful helpers, beloved friends

Cover Photo by Owen Brown

ISBN 0-590-31719-9

12 11 10 9 8 7 6 5 4 3 2 1   11   1 2 3 4 5 6/8

Printed in the U.S.A.   06

I DON'T WANT TO BE YOUR *SHADOW*

A Wishing Star Book

WISHING STAR TITLES
FROM SCHOLASTIC

1.

I SAT in my mother's Queen Anne chair, the one embroidered with roses and leaves of English ivy, listening to Sibelius on the stereo: *The Swan of Tuonela*. Outside, snow fell on the juniper trees; a lady cardinal darted for the last of the wild birdseed.

There was a fire — piñon wood, the rarest-smelling wood in the world. People catch its scent and ache, it is so beautiful. It reminds me of the smoke that wends its way from adobe chimneys in the Sangre de Cristo mountains. Ashy. Darkly pungent.

Full of memory.

For weeks and weeks, when the piñon has burned, I've thought: Jon. I look at the flames, scarlet and tangerine intertwining, and recall the times we held each other that way. It was innocent holding. Chaste. But for all its limits, his touch was powerfully affecting. To this day, when I think about it, my skin warms of its own accord.

We listened to Sibelius together, Jon and I — and Vivaldi, Purcell, Haydn. We listened to Linda Ronstadt, too — *Long, Long Time* — and Willie and Waylon, the Texas outlaws. Their Austin sound.

When we were in no mood to listen to others, we sang the songs that Jon had composed himself — strange lyrics that dipped and veered into minor strains. He wrote about love a lot, and it didn't occur to me until much later that his songs were all about love lost.

I was far too interested in love found. The love I felt for him burned in the pit of my stomach, twisting there. I wrote *Jon* in my notebooks, saw Jon in my dreams.

There was my mother worrying: "Wait! Don't get serious!" And Jon himself saying, "We'd better not get too serious. We're awfully young. There's college yet to come."

What do you say to things like that? Don't worry, I'm not serious, is what I said. Everyone's faces relaxed at that, and I could read their thoughts as clearly as if tickertape were spewing from their heads.

Sensible girl. She'll be all right.

But I wasn't sensible, and even today I'm not sure I'm all right. Not in the way I was before I met Jon. Or, for that matter, before I saw him.

Santa Fe is like Paris, the oldtimers say. If you wait long enough, sipping coffee at the outdoor cafes, the world will come to your door. And it does: in season, the tourists sound like twittering flocks of wild birds, pointing out landmarks and conversing in French, Spanish, German, Dutch. They emerge from Greyhound buses and small autos with European plates, to eat the hot chile rellenos, and to walk through the old adobe churches and stores. The oldest house in the United States is not far from where we live. And surrounding it all are the mountains: the Jemez, the Sandias, the Sangre de Cristos . . . everywhere you look, mountains folding in on the town like a mother's warm arms.

As the swallows return to Capistrano year after year, the tourists descend on Santa Fe. The year-round residents love them and hate them. They need the tourist money; they want tourists to buy their opera tickets, ski lift passes, souvenirs. But while the tourists are here, the town is lost to us. You cannot sit on the plaza and feed the pigeons without stumbling into travelers with cameras around their necks and questions on their faces. *Where's Guadalupe Street? You live here or just traveling like us? Where's the Oldest House? Where's the street where all the artists live? Where's Canyon Road?*

Sometimes I help them. Sometimes, when I'm out of the mood to help, I pretend not to be able to speak English. I make up some gibberish that sounds just like Italian, and sometimes I speak that. I was doing that the day I first saw Jon. A fat woman and her fat husband had cornered me just outside the French Pastry Shop. The woman still

3

had crumbs on her enormous bosom, and she wanted to know where the Roadrunner Tour tickets were sold.

I gesticulated like the Romans I had seen in films at the Collective Fantasy, and began to jabber away in my phony Italian. Then I saw a tall, lean boy staring with a puzzled expression at me from across the street. I had this idea that he knew what I was doing, which was ridiculous. He was too far away to hear. Still, it made me ashamed.

The fat woman, by then, had begun to huff and puff. She pushed on her sunglasses and pulled at her husband, very nervous all of a sudden. Maybe she thought I was crazy instead of Italian. Or maybe she spoke fluent Italian and thought I was Lithuanian, I don't know.

While the worried couple backed away, the tall boy continued to stare at me. I looked past him, into the shop window just behind, at a reflection of myself. It was one of those times when I was far from perfectly put-together, but I knew that disheveled or not, I was attractive to him. My face and arms were as brown as nutshells from summer and winter hikes in the Sangres, and my hair was tied in a pseudo-French knot, the kind that my mother wears. I was wearing my turquoise earrings — turquoise is supposed to bring good luck — and my Santa Fe Opera tee-shirt, which was beginning to swell and shrink in the proper places, after years of lying as flat as an old-fashioned ironing board.

If I have one notable feature, it is my eyes. They are enormous and dark and dominate my

4

face like charcoal insets, even without makeup. The reflection of my eyes was prominent, compensating for a too-small nose and too-wide mouth.

As I watched, the boy — who would later become Jon but for then was just an intensely interesting tourist type — turned around and glanced in the window himself. For a moment, our images mingled there. His arm seemed to touch my arm, our shoulders merged. Then two older people, his parents, I supposed, walked over to meet him. He smiled, showed them a package he'd bought in one of the stores, and they moved away. I stood there for a long time, watching the three of them walk toward St. Francis Cathedral: two tall, healthy-looking adults and their handsome son.

2.

WHEN I think of my early life, my life before Jon Purcell came into it, it seems to me that the very early days were the best.

When I was seven years old, my mother drove from our neighborhood in northern Santa Fe to a small village named Abiqui, not far from Española.

There we stopped at the General Store, where mother bought black coffee, no sugar, for herself, and a cold Dr Pepper for me. She fiddled with the coffee, tasting it and wrinkling her elegantly powdered nose. Then she asked for directions to the house of the famous artist, Georgia O'Keeffe.

The old woman's home turned out to be across the street from the store, though it was hidden from view by a depression in the ground and a large, opaque fence.

"She don't like gawkers much," the counter man warned.

Mother whiffed disdainfully against her dark glasses, rubbed them on her Irish sweater, and said, "It's all right. We're expected."

"You are," he droned, in a sure-you-are voice.

"That's right. Have you ever heard of Strong Gallery?"

"Sure, I heard. In Santa Fe."

"Well," she said, sliding her dark glasses up a sharp, businesslike nose. "That's gratifying. I'm Strong."

That exchange between them lingered in my mind, as did the rest of that remarkable day. I got to meet Georgia O'Keeffe, the way I met all of my mother's artists, but I didn't know what to make of her. Greatness showed on her as clearly as her age, which was advanced. She talked business and gossiped with my mother, the two of them reminiscing about friends in New York and New Mexico.

That left me to stare at O'Keeffe's apprentice, Juan Hamilton. He was many years younger than she, a tall man with dark hair that fell down his back. When I wouldn't take my eyes off him, he crossed his own in a crazy way.

Then, as I bit my tongue to hold back laughter, he fixed them right and went on listening to his teacher and my mother.

When the meeting drew to a close, I said what I had been coached to say ("I love your paintings, Miss O'Keeffe"), but that turned out to be a mistake.

"Do you, child?" she said in an absentminded voice. "What could you know of my painting, at your age?"

I know she didn't mean to be unkind. She'd just gotten sick of people telling her they loved her all the time. Maybe if I'd said I hated her, that would have sounded more sincere. I didn't have the courage.

That's far behind me now, but I bring it up to show how Mother always dragged me everywhere. *Lois's monkey,* the artists nicknamed me, as if we were an organ grinder show, with Mother the human part of the act.

They weren't far wrong in those days. Lots of times I would have preferred hanging around the house, watching television, or playing with my friends. But Mother was determined to "educate" me. To her, that meant cramming art, artists, and her art gallery down my throat, almost from the moment I was born.

"What's the trouble?" she asked after we left Abiqui and O'Keeffe and headed back to Santa Fe.

I tried to explain how awful I felt, how like a fifth wheel, and why. But as usual, she would have none of it.

"Goodness, Blake," she scolded. That's something else she did to me — that name. It is no name for a girl. In fact, it referred to her favorite poet, *William* Blake, but she wanted to name me something that would draw attention, stand out in a crowd. To my sorrow, it has. "Don't mind her. The woman's a genius. That's just the way she is. Of course she's different from anyone else. You have to make allowances for geniuses, learn to enjoy their little tics and quirks. It's all just part of the game."

9

She said that with such seriousness that I knew she deeply meant it. It might have been the credo of her life.

I can't remember when Mother wasn't playing the supremely confident, utterly poised and successful Lois Strong. Even her name sounded like two sharp blows from a hammer. She dressed in raw silk from Origins, lunched at the Periscope or whatever new place was making waves in Santa Fe, bought her first-edition art books from Applegate's Villagra, and warehoused me at trendy Montessori schools.

Every summer, she brought me into the gallery. "This is my daughter, Blake Cannaberry — Peter's, yes. Oh, back in Cambridge, I guess. No, never. Well, it's better that way, don't you think? Saves wear and tear on the nerves."

Translated, that means that my father was mother's second (and last) husband, an English art historian who fled for home after the marriage broke up, never to be heard from again. I can't remember a thing about him, though I'd like to. Peter. Peter Cannaberry. His name sounds so harmless, like a Christmas pudding with cranberries. Or maybe that's Mother's assessment, not mine.

The few times I asked about my father, she said, "Peter? Peter was perfectly harmless. Nothing wrong with him at all."

There was an edge of sorrow to her voice that made me wonder what exactly had passed between them.

I never pressed the point, never pinned my mother down, because I didn't want to make her unhappy. I know that sounds weird . . . admitting that you really love your mother, and want things to be easy for her. But I happen to feel that way about mine. I can't help it. She's not perfect by a long shot, but she may be the next-thing-to.

In the art world, my mother is almost a national treasure. Evidently, when my father took off, all she had were some paintings she'd bought cheaply from artist friends. Her friends, fortunately, were getting famous, so she was able to trade their work for money, or more paintings. Before anyone knew what was happening, she'd opened a small, very busy gallery in New York. Her instincts were so sharp that investors loved to back her. Buying my mother's opinions was like buying stock from ITT.

Then, just as her life in Manhattan was getting secure, she got excited about art in the West. She picked up a series of Indian lithographs at an auction, wanted more, and flew on a scouting trip to Santa Fe.

She never returned home after that. Friends closed up the New York apartment, which got sublet in a hurry. Her paintings were packed, insured for travel, and flown into Albuquerque, an hour's drive south of Santa Fe.

In two months, she had converted an old office supply store off the Santa Fe Plaza to a light, spacious gallery, where she proceeded to make a fortune and bring me up.

All without a husband, the newspapers loved to point out.

All by herself.

Somewhere in those stories, there was always a

mention of me. I am the handicap she overcame; the millstone around her career.

"I expect Blake to follow me into the business," Ms. Strong confides. "We're cut from the same cloth. She's a natural."

Those are always Mother's favorite words, and the words I hate the most. Cut from the same cloth? A natural what? Some days that seems flattering. Other days, the thought of following in her footsteps makes me aghast.

Sometimes, when I look in a mirror, the lines of my face seem to dissolve into hers.

We have the same chin, the same hair, the same (she would say "penetrating") eyes.

It's as if I never had a father at all — as if Peter Cannaberry were just an empty name. Which he is. You don't want it to be that way; if you have a father, you like to know things about him. But if you don't see him for years and years, he becomes a photograph and a set of letters oddly arranged.

When that happens, all you have in the world is what that father has left behind.

And that was my mother. Always, my mother.

3.

WE have almost a thousand mystery novels in our house. When Mother isn't working she likes to relax with an Agatha Christie or Ngaio Marsh whodunit.

If the phone rings, or someone comes to the door, books get left in the most bizarre places — the rim of the bathtub, the top of the refrigerator, behind a hanging cactus plant. They never get picked up again until weekly maid service comes, or someone's invited for dinner. Then Mother does it herself, crawling around on her hands and knees until everything is straight and in place.

When I walked in from the Washington Branch Library, where I'd been researching an overdue report on "Northern New Mexico: Land of Enchantment," Mother was scurrying like a laboratory rat in search of a treat.

It was an old pattern. Vacuumed floor. Books up. A mushroom quiche smelling up the kitchen.

13

"Who's coming for dinner?" I said.

Mother crammed three mysteries onto an already full shelf, then collapsed in a chair. "Strangers. No one you know."

"Artists?"

"Not tonight. These people are the " — she put her hand over her eyes as if she couldn't quite remember the name — "*Purcells*, that's it."

"Customers?"

"Friends of your Aunt Holly," she said. "They're moving to Santa Fe from Fort Lauderdale. Came into the gallery today — cold. No warning at all. Stayed until I invited them to dinner. Which, by the way, I could kill myself for."

"Why'd you do it, then?"

She whipped out a Dunhill cigarette and said, "Because I'm stupid, that's why. Throw me a match?"

I threw.

"Thanks, Blake." Inhaling seemed to relax her. Mother is one of those people who screams non-stop about the perils of teenage smoking, then can't wait to light up herself. She coughed in a spasm, recovered, and said, "This will be of interest to you. Mr. and Mrs. Fort Lauderdale have a son your age."

"What's his name?"

"John. No, what did his mother say — not John with *h*, just J-O-N, Jon."

"What's he like?"

She shrugged, massaged the skin underneath her wristwatch. "Absolutely no idea. He was hacking around the plaza, that's Kay Purcell's

14

term, *hacking around*, so I didn't get a look. If he's anything like his father, he looks like a golf pro. A sweater person. All scrubbed and woolly, if you like that sort of thing."

"Did they like the gallery?"

"How could they? They didn't know what it was. I can recognize good art people in a minute. This woman probably has a Woolworth print of *The Blue Boy* hanging in her house. Oh, that's tacky. What's wrong with me today? I didn't mean it." Her lips drew up in a grin. "She probably has Van Gogh's *Sunflowers*. The big time."

"You're an awful snob, you know it? Just full of vinegar today."

"True. Well, *a*, I don't want to eat with strangers tonight, just my own kid, and *b*, those etchings from Nambe haven't come in. I'm going to go crazy with this place, you know it?"

"You could always go back to New York."

She blinked without humor. "No."

"No, huh?"

She threw a needlepoint pillow across the room, barely missing me. "What a smart mouth! What did I do to deserve such a smart mouth?" I threw the pillow back. "Everything I learned, I learned from you, you know. . . ."

We were still throwing pillows, playing the game, when the doorbell sounded. Mother shut her eyes.

"It can't be them. I have no makeup on, no perfume."

"What time did you tell them to come?"

"Six," Mother said. She checked her watch.

"It's six now. Look, can you handle them? Bartend? Just pour them some chablis, that's all they get. And I'll be right back, okay?"

"Okay."

Over her shoulder, she yelled, "No wine for you! None!"

"Why not?"

"Because," she called, disappearing into her room, "they're Aunt Holly's friends. And you know your Aunt Holly."

I opened the door and bit my tongue, not to laugh. Mother's description was wickedly on-the-mark. Mr. Purcell did look like a golf pro, exactly, and Mrs. Purcell could have been wearing a sign: Aunt Holly's Garden Club Pal. As alien from our usual friends as they seemed, there was something disturbingly familiar about them.

They smiled like Florida sunshine. Almost blinded by a flash of white teeth, I let them in.

"You must be Lois's girl," Mrs. Purcell said. She handed me her sweater and said, "My, my."

Mr. Purcell pumped my hand and said, "Nice place. Lois do this by herself?"

"The decorating, you mean?"

He nodded.

"No. She had some help. She was too busy to decorate when she bought the house."

"I wish you wouldn't ask questions like that, Dad."

I turned to get a better look at Jon, and all the missing pieces of the puzzle fell into place. He was the same lanky boy I'd seen earlier downtown. He must have recognized me, too, for he flushed and averted his eyes, then lifted them to

16

meet mine in a sheepish gaze. He must have known I'd caught him looking at me. But then, I'd been eyeing at him from in front of the Pastry Shop, as guilty of staring as he.

"Pardon me," Mr. Purcell said with exaggerated regret. "Blake, does your mother embarrass you to death?"

"In what way?"

"Like asking about decorating? Things like that?"

I had trouble focusing on what he meant. "No, not at all."

"That's a shame," he grunted. "I was hoping it was a teenage thing. Something all of you went through."

"Like the measles?" I went to the bar and poured glasses of white wine, as my mother had specified. Mr. and Mrs. Purcell were just as healthy-looking inside as they had been out. They were the sort of people one would expect to see dangling a tennis racket from their hands.

They took the glasses and sipped. "Where's your mother, anyway?" Mrs. Purcell finally said.

"She's around. She'll be here in a second."

"She's here right now." Mother draped herself in the doorway, the way actresses used to do in those old black-and-white television shows. "So you found the house?"

"Your directions were very good."

"Good. It's good that they were good."

"Well, they were. *Really* good," Mrs. Purcell chatted nervously. "In fact, they couldn't have been much better. The way you told us, Greg knew right where to go."

I glanced at Jon, who was as pained by the awkward exchange as I was. A pulse jumped in his cheek, betraying tension. While our parents were talking, he wandered over to the library shelves and ran his hands over the bindings. I decided to follow him.

"You like to read?" I asked.

"Love it."

"What do you read?"

He shrugged. "Everything. Turgenev and Tolstoy — I like Russian novels. Poetry. Science fiction. You name it."

I was impressed by the offhand way he reeled off the categories, and by the steady way he met my eyes. "You're really serious about reading, are you?"

A faint smile crossed his face. "Santa Feans aren't the only literate people in the world, you know. We used to read quite a lot in Fort Lauderdale. Books, real books, when we couldn't get the funnies."

A flush crept across my face. He had a point. Santa Fe is an artistic and literary community, and the people who live here do have inflated opinions of their own intelligence and talent. That's what my mother always says. She adds that that's a very good thing. When people want to look smart, they buy expensive art for their walls. They buy it from her, usually.

"Look, I didn't mean . . ." I said.

"It's okay," he assured me, moving toward another shelf. "You're mother's a sophisticated lady. I heard Mom and Dad talking about her on

18

the way over here. She's accomplished a lot, and I'm impressed. I don't know a thing about art. But I'm not a hick." He gestured toward his parents. "Neither are they. Regular people have something to offer to the world, too, you know."

"What do you mean, regular people?"

"Fathers who work at normal jobs. Mothers who stay at home to be mothers. That kind of thing."

Quickly, he moved to join them.

For the rest of the evening, I tried maneuvering to talk to him alone. Dinner didn't go well. My mother doesn't realize it, but she has two sets of manners. Both sets are perfectly fine, but one she saves for people she'd like to see again; the other she uses on people who don't particularly interest her.

She was using the second set now. And the worst of it was, the Purcells didn't know. They kept talking away about Fort Lauderdale, the canal there, and Aunt Holly's famous Florida room, which is draped with so many ferns you practically have to hack your way through it with a machete. Mother's eyes were attentive, but glazed. Probably, she was doing accounting in her head.

". . . so I thought, Blake could take Jon around the town, show him where things are, since we'll be living here," Mrs. Purcell was saying.

Mother snapped to. "I'm sorry?"

"Blake and Jon. I thought the two of them could go downtown tomorrow. So Jon could get his bearings here."

"Oh, I don't know," Mother said.

It was the opening I'd been waiting for. I swallowed slowly and thought fast.

"I'd like that," I said. "I really would."

"See?" Mrs. Purcell said.

Mother frowned. "If you're sure, Blake. You've got that report, don't forget."

"It's finished."

"Well . . ."

"I want to. Really, or I wouldn't have said." I grinned at Jon — so much haggling over a little thing. He relaxed and smiled back, exposing a small cleft at the tip of his chin. Until that moment, I had been sure that only film stars had them. My heart turned over.

"Hmmmm," Mother said with poor grace. "That's settled, then." She reached for a crystal carafe and carefully began to pour. When all five glasses were filled, she looked around brightly and forced a smile. "Greg . . . Kay? And Jon, of course. Want a tour of some small sculpture I've been storing?"

It sounded like a question, but I knew, we all knew, that it wasn't.

"Sure," Jon said, which was the only possible answer.

Following behind her, we all filed into the den.

4.

JON agreed to meet me at Geppetto's, a small hot chocolate and hamburger shop right off the plaza, because that was the only place he could remember how to find. I don't think he wanted to meet me at all. He seemed to find me uninteresting and didn't have much to say for the rest of the evening. But his mother bullied him into joining me, and after a few minutes of resistance, he agreed to come.

I wondered if he had changed his mind, after all. He was late, first just a few minutes, then he grew very late. I bought a cup of hot chocolate and sat down by myself, feeling very self-conscious. I hadn't brought anything to read and there was no newspaper rack nearby. So I had to sip my chocolate and look out the window, as if I were happy having nothing to do and nobody in the world to talk to.

Some people don't mind waiting around alone

21

in public. My mother is like that. She can sit in a restaurant all by herself and look as if she has every right in the world to be there. She doesn't hide behind newspapers, either. She people-watches, sips her coffee, and is able to relax. Sometimes she jokes with waiters or calls out to someone she knows at another table.

I'm just the opposite. If I'm not in a group, I feel embarrassed. Don't ask me why — I know it's senseless. But I've finally quit fighting it. It's just the way I am.

I was wanting to crawl into a hole by this time. All around me, couples and threesomes were eating egg and chile sandwiches. I felt like the only animal on the Ark without a partner. Thinking about that, wondering what in the world could be keeping Jon, I drank too much of the scalding cocoa. It blistered my tongue and settled in my stomach about as comfortably as molten lava.

Then I tipped the cup over and spilled some on my jeans. It didn't show on the denim, but I could feel the skin on my leg redden and grow sore. I was trying to soak up some of the chocolate with a paper napkin when Jon finally put in an appearance. I was beginning to feel upset by then. He was almost twenty minutes late and the chocolate had burned me so badly that I had almost no feeling in my tongue.

But these things seemed unimportant when he smiled, waved, and walked up to give his own order. While it was filled, he flashed me a "just a minute" sign. I stopped rubbing my leg, which had quit hurting anyway, and stared at him.

Not many boys look like Jon Purcell. He is one

of these people who has perfect teeth without orthodontia, who has thick hair with no cow-licks, who shoot up past six feet without looking like the string of a yo-yo. I don't know if you could say that he is Film Star handsome, but in some ways he is better than that — he looks like a normal person with no perceptible flaws.

I have a pleasant enough face, but I've never been very secure about my looks because Mother and her friends are always saying, "Blake's going to grow into a beauty someday." That leaves the problem of what Blake is now. Someday is still a few years off, it would seem, and I am the sort of person who wants everything good to happen right away.

I sat a little straighter as Jon came over. He slid another cup of cocoa in front of me.

"I'm late," he apologized.

"Were you? I didn't notice," I lied.

"Oh, yes. I'm a good" — he checked his wrist-watch — "fifteen minutes behind. I overslept, then my mother made me clean my room. And my father asked me to stack some firewood before I took off."

"Do they always make you work like that?"

"Always," he said, and grinned. " 'Jon Purcell, get in here this minute and straighten up this room! It looks like mold growing on cheese.' "

We both laughed at his falsetto, which was a great imitation of Mrs. Purcell. Then he grew more sober.

"How about you?" he asked. "Does your mother make you do a lot around the house?"

"Not really."

"She does it all?"

"She doesn't do anything, unless things get really messy after the maid leaves. A few times a year she calls in a service for heavy cleaning. The rest of the time, her regular cleaning people do it."

"Must be nice," he said.

"Well, I guess. Sure, it is."

"Is she a good cook, your mother?"

"She's a lousy cook," I admitted. "Every time company comes in, we have Michael's Quiche. Michael's Quiche, Michael's Quiche. I mean, it's good, but I'm sick of it. And for dessert, Pink Adobe apple pie, so she can just stick it in the oven. Even so, it gets burned sometimes."

"You're joking."

"I'm serious. When would she have time to cook? She's always at the gallery, or on buying trips, or seeing people. We eat out a lot. Restaurant food is all right. And there's a good sandwich shop around the block when we have to rush."

"That's not very — " He struggled for a word, finally settled on, "*homey,* is it?"

"I don't know," I said. "Depends on what you mean by homey. Look, if you're through with your cocoa, I'll show you around. I thought we'd walk over to Alameda River Park after we do the plaza. That way, you'll see a good section of downtown."

He smiled and reached across the table for my jacket, which he helped me get into, an arm at a time. When we got to the door, I couldn't help noticing that he hurried to open it for me and that he took the street-side of the sidewalk without seeming to think about it.

It was as if he were from another planet, instead of Fort Lauderdale — or another time, instead of the present.

People say that Santa Fe is more a European city than an American one. It's very old-feeling here. Our buildings are made from adobe and seem to rise from the earth like miniature hills, so that you don't have any sensation of metal and glass intruding upon the landscape. The town is surrounded by high, almost-blue mountains, which stay capped with snow except during the summer. Everywhere you look, there are pine and juniper trees, which seem twisted and biblical; it smells like a Christmas tree lot after it rains or snows.

The finest thing of all is the sky. The air in northern New Mexico is clear and tart; sunsets are so beautiful that every night people go outside, lean from their balconies, or sit on their porches until darkness comes. In grocery stores and on the plaza, you hear, "Did you see the one last night?" — meaning the sunset — as often as "How's the family?"

But there are drawbacks to living here, too. The air is thinner than other places, and until newcomers get used to it, they have to walk slowly and sleep more than usual. Jon didn't know this, and seemed embarrassed when he ran out of breath and had to walk like an arthritic old man. His face was drawn with pain; his lungs seemed about to explode. When we finally reached Alameda, he flung himself on the banks of the river and looked at me with a rueful grin.

"I'm usually not — "

"Don't worry about it."

Our voices collided, causing us to laugh. I explained about the altitude, and how it would take time before he could expect to feel as strong as he had before.

"I wondered about that," he said. "The other day, before we came to your house for dinner — I was feeling sluggish then."

"You fooled me."

"Good. I meant to." He picked a piece of grass and peeled its stem. "It's really strange here, Blake. *Good* strange, but . . . I don't know, just different. I'm beginning to wonder if I'll ever feel at home."

"Of course you will."

"I'm not so sure." He threw the blade of grass into the water and watched it float away. "I liked Fort Lauderdale a lot. My school, my friends. A bunch of us used to go the beach every single weekend."

"Was there a girlfriend?" I asked.

"Sure. Of course."

I was sorry I'd asked, but now that I had, I was curious to hear more. "You must miss her a lot. I guess that's why you're sorry to be in Santa Fe."

"I didn't say I was sorry to be here. I just said it felt strange. As for Pam . . ."

"That was her name?"

"Pam King," he said. "You would have liked her a lot. She was a terrific person. But her father was an officer in the Army, and she moved to

Germany about two months before we moved here. So that was all over."

Neither of us spoke for a long time. I didn't offer any information about my romantic past. The fact is, I don't have one.

It's not as if I've felt superior to all that, either. The opportunity has simply never arisen. Not one boy has ever professed his deep and abiding love for me. One or two have complimented me on my wonderful mind, and while I like that, it's about as romantic as a case of trench mouth. I often dream of the day when the opposite sex will look at me and realize what fools they have been, and what a blooming geranium of a girl I am.

My mother is afraid I have trouble getting a boyfriend because of her broken marriage. The first time she said that to me, I had to really stop and think what she meant.

Then she explained: Perhaps I was traumatized by the early loss of my father and had learned to distrust men. I don't really believe that, but it sounds better than other excuses. When I feel most depressed about not having a romantic past, and possibly no chance of a romantic future, I chalk it up to childhood trauma. It's a face-saving thing. Nothing wrong with that.

Behind us, people were spreading a picnic. A large Doberman bounded past, glad to be free of its leash. I closed my eyes and tried to imagine what a girl named Pam King would look like. Beautiful, probably. As beautiful as Jon.

I was fighting a tight, sad feeling in my chest when I noticed Jon was watching me closely.

"What's wrong?" he said.

"Nothing."

"Nothing?"

"That's right."

His eyes widened as if in disbelief. Then he said, "How would you like to go out with me Saturday?"

I raised an eyebrow. "Just like that?"

"People do that here, don't they?" he hedged. "Go out? Do things together?"

"Sometimes they do. When they like each other."

"Well, we do, don't we? Like each other. So we should go out, don't you think?"

He made it sound so easy, so sensible, that I buried thoughts of Fort Lauderdale girls and said yes. It was why I had wanted to see him today, after all. I hadn't admitted that before, not even to myself, but this was exactly what I'd wanted to happen.

As if he were a mind reader, he reached over and gave my hand a squeeze. On the other side of the river, a little boy was struggling to raise a purple bat kite. The breeze wouldn't lift it. It crashed into a tree.

"Oh, the memories," Jon groaned. "Can you remember when you smashed your first kite?"

But I was concentrating on other things.

Saturday, I thought.

28

5.

IT would have been all right if I had not seen
Jon until that weekend, but once he had actually asked me out, I began to run into him all the
time. I wondered if that had been the case all
along: if he had been there, if we had seen each
other (twice? many times?), and if, not knowing
him, I had simply not registered his presence.

He was often with his parents, one or both,
usually just with his mother. They were always
talking together, she doing more listening than
talking, her head cocked to the side as if everything her son said was of intense interest to her.

One afternoon, I saw them sitting together in
the French Pastry Shop. I had gone to buy
croissants for my mother's Saturday brunch, so I
had an excuse to walk in and wave at their table.
Mrs. Purcell looked up from her cup and smiled.
She nudged Jon and motioned for me to come
over.

"Look who's here," she said when I was in earshot. Then, speaking directly to Jon, she repeated, "Look who's here. Isn't this nice? Sit down, Blake. Come on, surely you can spare a moment for us?"

I wasn't sure that I could. I'd promised my mother I would help her put mailing stickers on catalogues that afternoon. She was so desperate for help that she'd actually promised to pay me to do it.

But Mrs. Purcell was insistent. It crossed my mind that she was lonely. That, or she was worried about Jon being lonely.

"Please stay," she said. "For just a little while, anyway. Waitress? Can you bring another cup?"

"Oh, no," I told her. "Honestly, I — "

"Bring another cup," she repeated before I could protest further. "What do you want to drink, Blake, coffee or cocoa?"

"They have good teas," I said, relenting.

"That's fine, then. Bring a cup of tea. No, bring a pot."

Throughout all this, Jon had not said a word. Finally, though, he smiled and said, "We just came from the Army surplus store."

"What for?"

"Backpacking equipment," he said. "Really, just a day pack. A big enough pack for some water and dried fruit, that's all we need. I thought I'd hike up the ski run Sunday."

"Have you ever done that?" Mrs. Purcell asked.

"Once."

"How was it?"

"Steep," I admitted. "I had a hard time.

Couldn't have done it without a walking stick, but that's just me. Better hikers do fine up there. I wouldn't take a dog, though, if I were you."

"Why?"

"The friend I was hiking with almost lost his. Dogs go wild up there. Maybe it's the thin air, I don't know. Lots of people bring dogs, but I still don't think it's a good idea."

"Oh," Mrs. Purcell said. "Well, Jon doesn't own a dog, so that's no problem."

My tea arrived then, and the waitress asked whether I wanted cream or lemon.

"Try it with cream," Mrs. Purcell suggested. "That's the way the English take theirs. It's good with cream."

"My parents went to England last summer," Jon said.

"Did you go, too?"

"No. I stayed with my grandmother instead."

We talked about England for a while, then I got nervous about my mother expecting me.

"I'm glad you and Jon are getting together," Mrs. Purcell told me before I left. "He needs to know people here. And besides, you'll enjoy it. He's not bad company."

"She hopes," Jon joked.

"She knows," Mrs. Purcell said.

I thanked her for the tea, and went to the counter to buy croissants. There were only half a dozen left, so I bought them all. When I left, Jon and his mother were thick in conversation.

I thought about that all the way to the gallery: about how it would be to have a mother who could spend that kind of time with you, just talking and drinking coffee like that, not running off to buy art and sell it. I tried to imagine my mother saying something like, "Blake's not bad company," but it was hard. She might think that, but I couldn't imagine her saying it.

So that's what a real mother is like, I found myself thinking. All the time in the world for you, saying good things about you.

I jammed the bag of croissants into my windbreaker and broke into a run, muttering excuses out of the corner of my mouth as I dodged people on the sidewalk.

Several more times before Saturday, I saw Jon. He was trying to learn his schedule at school and was still making false turns, so he was highly visible.

And once more I caught a glimpse of the two of them, Jon and his mother, getting into their car in front of a shopping center. The car was loaded with grocery bags and green houseplants. Jon had to squeeze into the front seat, beside a large dracena plant that almost hid his mother's face from view. Something about that scene tapped aches that I didn't know I had: the normalcy of a driving mother picking up her son, the grocery bags, the plants selected to make a house warmer, more homelike.

The fact that Mrs. Purcell was doing these things herself particularly struck me.

I remembered when we had moved into our own house. Movers hauled the furniture, Plant World trucked the greenery, employees from the gallery hung our art, maids put the clothes and dishes away.

I thought it would be fun to arrange our own rooms, but Mother had a road show in Denver to plan. She hadn't promoted her artists in Denver before. When I tried to talk to her about placing beds and chests-of-drawers, she started muttering about art prices. If this show didn't sell out, how could she meet the mortgage payments?

The show did sell out, the house payments were met, and everything we owned got unpacked and put away. But it was less exciting somehow, than if we had done that ourselves. When I am grown and have my own house, everything in it will be arranged by me. I knew without asking that that was what Jon's mother was doing, what other women, the women I had begun to think of as "real mothers," would also do.

6.

MOTHER was gone when I returned from the library on Saturday afternoon, but she had left a note by the telephone:

Sweetheart —
I had to make a quick run to Taos to pick up some lithographs. *Will try to be home before your date!* If I'm running behind, help your-self to anything you need from my room — makeup, lotions, whatever. There is a piece of Michael's Crab Quiche in the refrigerator that will be delicious warmed up. I know that is your favorite.

I might stop off at Chamayo for dinner, but am feeling pretty tired — I'll be home early. Have a good time and tell Jon to drive *very* carefully. He's not used to so many one-way streets.

I love you!

Mother

For a minute, I really felt let down. I'd expected her to be home, helping me pick out things to wear, and telling me how great I looked. Sometimes it's good to have a high-powered career mother, and sometimes it's not.

I didn't worry about it long, though. There was too much else to do. I thought about wearing a dress, but that didn't seem like a good idea. I was afraid it would look a little anxious-to-impress. I went through my closet, and finally decided on a clean pair of jeans and my favorite red sweater, which had just come back from the cleaners.

I was brushing my hair with Mother's natural bristle brush, when she rushed into the house, breathless.

"Good! I didn't miss you," she said. "I was so afraid I would. There was this one odd-sized canvas that wouldn't go into the car. We tried every possible angle, and it absolutely wouldn't budge. So I thought, well, United Parcel. But of course, they were closed. . . ." She put down her purse, pulled off her sunglasses, and sighed. "Blake, forgive me for running on, but it's been *such* a day. Step out. Let me see how you look."

I did as she asked.

"You're beautiful. Of course, in my day, it would've been a dress, not jeans. But that sweater is marvelous . . . red is your color. I've been trying to persuade Alex Levine to paint you, but he wants you in brown against adobe. Earthtones . . ." Her voice trailed off.

"Alex painted me just last year."

"And sold the oil from under us! This one he's promised for me."

"I don't know. I don't enjoy sitting for him as much as some of your other friends."

"Why ever not?"

"He smokes while he's working," I said.

"So do I."

"Not a pipe. Not that tobacco of his."

"I thought you loved the smell of a pipe!"

I shrugged to show that she had a point, that in times past I had remarked on a pipe's good smell.

The truth was, I disliked Alex for quite another reason. He reminded me of Humbert Humbert in *Lolita*, with its story of an older man attracted to a young girl.

Alex Levine sometimes looked at me like that, as if he were wondering whether I had a sex life yet. At the time of the portrait-painting, I was too innocent to know how to stop him dead in his tracks. And also, I think, I had a horror that he would protest I'd misunderstood. (I knew I had not misunderstood a thing, but all he would have to do would be to say I had. I sensed that the burden of proof was overwhemingly on me — that people, even my own mother, would side with talented Alex and think that I had lied.)

"Not that it matters," Mother was saying now. "I've gone through periods of disliking certain smells myself. Once I was off my cologne — you remember that blend with the sandalwood base? And Juniper it was, another year. Juniper wood made me so allergic I thought I would die."

Before she could launch into a description of her allergy attacks, the doorbell rang. I grabbed my navy pea jacket on the way out the door, determined to flee with Jon before she could draw him inside and monopolize him.

I wanted us to be alone.

When I am an old, old woman counting memories (of Jon? of someone else?) I will always remember the first time I felt electricity between us. It happened by accident — his joke, my laugh, then our eyes catching, locking. His mouth trembled for no reason at all, then he reached over to lift a wisp of hair from my eyes.

It would have been natural to kiss then, but he did not kiss me. He looked away as if he had seen a fire. Then he turned the key in the ignition, slipped a cassette tape into the recorder, songs sung by *Clannad* that evoked visions of Irish wars and druids.

We drove high into the National Forest, up the Ski Basin road, which was clear of ice. No other cars passed ours. It was a good time to talk, but we were shy of that, as we had been shy of kissing earlier. So we listened to the music instead, and looked up at the pitch-black sky, where constellations glittered like cheap jewels in the tiara of a beauty queen.

I wanted to touch him, to hold his hand, to draw him closer to me. But I did none of those things. I just looked at the sky and listened to the songs change from one to another and wondered why love felt like such a tug, such a physical ache.

"Happy?" he said.

"Ummm."

"Ummm yes or ummm no?"

"Ummm."

He laughed then, delighted, and reached over to cover my hand with his own. When we reached a high overlook, he stopped the car; turned off the music. Said, "What's the good smell?"

"Piñon pine."

"Piñon . . . ?"

"That's right."

"I want to learn that. The names of the trees here — everything like that."

"Because you want to turn native?"

"Because I want some familiarity with things that are important to you."

I wanted to ask why but couldn't. It stuck in my throat. Somehow he had heard my unspoken question and answered.

"It just feels . . . like I should." He cracked the window and inhaled the foresty air. "I guess this is what's commonly referred to as 'parking.' Do you mind?"

I grinned, not minding a bit.

"We'll turn back in a minute," he promised. "But just think, Blake. Our parents must have done this once. This very thing — sat and talked. Wondered about the future."

Something of the moment lessened. "I cannot imagine my mother ever sitting in a car and talking about *anything* with my father. Except why no child support all these years, and why did he disappear."

"Surely they were in love once?"

"Not a chance."

"C'mon, Blake!"

"*You* come on! I'm telling you, you don't know my mother. She's passionate, all right, but every

39

drop of her passion goes into work. I know what I'm talking about. Every so often she'll meet a nice man, and I'll get all excited and think — you know — a stepfather. But then these men begin to want more of her time, for dates, dinners out, talks on the phone, and she gets this tight, pinched look and starts talking about how much her work means to her and how she can't let any-one interfere with it. She's serious, too. She loves that gallery as much as she loves me — maybe more. She says that it will still be there long after I go off to college and leave her alone."

"She really said that?"

I mimicked her. " 'You're going to leave for school soon enough darling, but don't worry about me. I'll always have my pictures.' "

Jon looked at me intently. "You're not much like her," he said.

"Now I'm not. I wonder about later."

"You'll never be like her. You're feminine."

"I don't know how to take that. You mean my mother's not?"

"She's beautiful. But there's something wrong with a woman who'd make her career her whole life."

"Lifework," I said.

"What?"

"Lifework. That's what she calls the gallery — her lifework."

"Well, then," he said, as if that were somehow a momentous piece of information. I felt he had passed a verdict on my mother, perhaps on the way the two of us lived, and I knew it was an unfavorable one. Even knowing that our opinions were the same, I somehow resented that.

Questions washed over me. What's the matter with her working hard if she's happy? Who cares if a *man* is slightly obsessed with a career? But we never got around to arguing about that.

Jon bent over to kiss me instead, and I found myself forgiving him, caught up in the enjoyment of kissing him back. Then the kiss began to feel dangerous, as if we were going someplace neither of us was prepared to go. Feeling uneasy, we parted and drove down the mountain, back into town.

I remembered that it was Bach Festival time in Santa Fe, and I knew of a corner of St. Francis Auditorium where we could listen to the musicians practice free. My mother had shown it to me years earlier, when a Chamber Music Festival was on and her gallery was obtaining posters for promotion.

We had a clear field that night — only three people labored on the stage. The rest of the musicians were mingling in the hall outside, packing their instruments to go home.

From time to time the practice stopped, and the conductor would lean over the podium and argue with the musicians, using extravagant gestures. Then the flautist and pianist would begin again, chilling me with the fluidity and precision of their efforts.

Jon hunched forward in concentration, his hands working restlessly in time with Bach's Suite in B minor. His face had an odd light to it, as if a wise man had told him a wondrous thing he had never heard before.

I think I began to wonder if I could love him then, sitting in the overlighted, cavernous room, intent on the Bach. He was Jon at his least beautiful. The fluorescence outlined pockets under his eyes; the beginnings of a shadow darkened his cheeks. He could not have been shaving long, for nick-marks were palely visible here and there on his face. But I liked that, too — the imperfection as well as the perfection.

We sat for a very long while, until the performers quit their instruments and went off. An aged janitor clattered his keys, letting us know that we were intruding there. When we finally did start for home, it seemed that just minutes had passed since our coming.

It was hard to send him away from our house, when we got there.

I wondered if it was hard for him to leave.

7.

MY mother looked like a girl, with hair wisping around her face and her makeup scrubbed off. She was rubbing her forehead, drinking black coffee, and balancing an unlit cigarette, her gestures following each other like exposures on fast film. When she saw me, she nudged an empty cup in my direction.

"Good time," she said.

"Good time?"

"With Jon. Last night."

"Oh," I said. "A very good time."

She nodded as if an oil painting had been hung exactly to her liking, then lit her cigarette.

"*How* good?"

"I told you. Very."

"That's not telling anything," she said. "Not really. I want details."

I poured myself some strong coffee and sat

down to face her. "I don't think I'm supposed to talk to you like that," I protested.

"Like what?"

"Like a friend. You're not my friend, you know. You're my mother. Those are two very different kinds of things."

"Oh," she said. "Perhaps they are."

I waited for her to say something else, but she didn't — not her. She reached for her copy of *Art News* and began to leaf through it, stopping when she came to an article on the Impressionists.

"We did hear a Bach rehearsal," I said.

"Did you? Did Jon like that?"

"He liked it a lot," I told her.

She put down the magazine and smiled at me, as I recounted everything I'd planned to withhold.

It always happened that way, her prodding, my retreating, then my telling her everything she'd wanted to know in the first place. She had that power over me — she still does.

It's a difficult thing to explain.

"So," she said, when I had finished relating everything I was going to, not everything, but almost everything, "interest runs high."

"What interest?"

"Your interest in this young man. Jon."

I shrugged to show it didn't really matter one way or another, but she wasn't fooled for a moment.

"Do it right, Blake," she said. "This is such an important time of life for you. So many people to meet. Be careful, and whatever you do, you want to do it right. You don't want to get infatuated this young."

44

She mashed her cigarette into an earthen ash-tray and looked out the window.

"You don't," she said again for emphasis.

Later that afternoon, the postman rang our bell.

"Registered for your mother," he said when I opened the door.

"She's not here."

"That's all right. You can sign."

I scribbled *Blake Cannaberry* on the green card he held out to me, then took the letter, which was written on very thin paper and postmarked Kensington. It was battered as if it had been a long time coming.

"That's not all," the postman said. "Here's your gas bill, here's your electric. A *New Mexican*. Let's see what else."

I waited.

"Nothing else," he said. "Say hello to Miss Strong for me, will you?"

"I will."

"Nice lady, your mother. She was good to me last Christmas."

"Me, too."

"Real good," he said. "That's why I bring the mail to the door some days instead of just to the box. Do you think she notices?"

"Some days she doesn't notice much."

"Maybe you could remind her, then. Do you think? Just tell her you saw me and that I brought the mail to the door instead of just to the box."

"All right," I promised. "I'll tell her tonight."

"You do that. If you don't mind."

"I don't mind," I said.

Because it was fair outside and I was restless, I decided to walk to the gallery and give my mother the letter by hand.

When I got there, she wasn't in. I was on my way out again when I saw her hurrying down East Palace with some rolled posters tucked under her arm.

"You're leaving?" her lips moved.

I hesitated by the door.

"Don't leave," I heard her call out.

She was breathless when she caught up with me.

"Here. Take these," she said, pushing the posters toward me. "They're for the Chamber Music Festival. Go on, unroll one and take a look. Aren't they terrific?"

"They're good."

"I think they're terrific," she said. "You never did overstate, even as a child. 'Good,' you say."

" 'Good' is a good word."

"Oh, Blake." She pushed hair out of her face and fumbled for a cigarette.

"Look," I said. "This came for you. I don't know what it is, maybe something from a friend. I thought you'd want it."

She took the letter and turned it curiously in her hands. As I watched, her face worked in a strange way.

"What is it?" I asked.

"You don't know his handwriting. You don't even know his handwriting."

"Whose?"

"Your father's," she said.

I felt as if a truck had run over me. It was hard

to breathe, really hard, as if I had been hyperventilating during exercise. My hands felt warm where the envelope had lain.

My mother ripped the letter open and moved her mouth as she read. It seemed like a short letter. In just a few minutes she had finished it, though her eyes still rested on the page.

"What did he have to say?" I asked in a voice that sounded thin and unlike my own.

"Do you want to read it?"

"Sure," I said. But something held me back. "I guess I want to. Would it be all right?"

"I offered, didn't I?"

I took the letter and began to read. I tried to imagine his voice as I read, what it would sound like saying the words that he had written. I wondered if it were a deep voice or just a tenor one. He would have an English accent, but perhaps not much of one, because of those years in New York. I tried to imagine, too, his hands as they held the pen: perhaps they were hands like mine, with long, tapered fingers that flared out like a nimbus, and flat palms. My hands looked nothing like my mother's. Perhaps they were Cannaberry hands.

Dear Lois [he wrote],
It was gratifying to get your letter and the news of Blake. Of course she would be intelligent and pretty. I never envisioned her any other way.

Thank you for asking about my work. It's interesting. I'm writing forewords to art books for a London publishing firm, and I also write display copy for several museums on a freelance basis. I'm trying to get a book together on the Surrealists, but it's difficult to find the time. I also discovered that a publishing house in Switzerland had done a similar project last year, which blunted my interest. It's hard to discipline myself to do anything for long. I guess you remember that trait of mine.

No, I haven't remarried. Have you? Sometimes I want to and sometimes I don't.

I have carefully weighed your suggestion that Blake visit me here this summer. Please tell her that I'd like that very much, but that it will be impossible for many reasons. I don't expect you to understand this, but perhaps she will. I imagine she's a highly perceptive girl . . .

I put the letter down, unfinished.

"You asked him to let me visit?" I said.

"Some time ago. Months ago."

"*Why?*"

She suddenly looked tired. "Because he's your father. I thought you should know him, that's all."

"But he's never written me. I didn't think you even knew where he was!"

"I didn't for a long time," she told me, and began to explain. When they divorced there was bitterness: she thought she never wanted to see him again. He disappeared in England for years. She would hear stories about him but had no way of knowing whether they were true. She heard that he had made a lot of money; then she heard from another source that he was poor, that there was no money at all. She heard that he had married and had other children, and she heard that he was single and always would be.

So she put him out of her mind as much as she could, until she took a buying trip to New York. She walked into a gallery and there he was, looking at pictures.

At first, she was not sure that it was him. He had aged and softened. So she followed him for a moment, until he must have sensed her eyes on him and turned around. Then she knew.

"Hello," he said. Here my mother's voice grew tense, and I had no trouble envisioning the scene: the two of them sizing each other up, not knowing whether to be friendly or cold. Friendly must have won, because they went out for coffee and talked about their lives and me for the rest of the afternoon. At some point, he suggested that my mother send me to England for a while, and she had agreed. They traded cards, like two salesmen on the road, which is how he got our address. Then my mother suggested a date for my visit.

And my father had said no. For many reasons, he had said no.

"Why do you think he doesn't want me to come?" I asked.

She shrugged. "It would be painful for him. Seeing what he missed out on—that kind of thing."

"Maybe he doesn't have the money?"

"I offered to buy the ticket, Blake." My mother

ducked her head, possibly ashamed of having told me that. It wouldn't have hurt her to let me think it was a matter of finances.

I bunched my jacket together and headed for the door, my heart hanging in my chest like iron.

"Where are you going?" my mother demanded.

"I don't know."

"I don't think you should run off like this," she said. "Without talking more. Don't you want to stay and talk?"

"I wish we hadn't talked in the first place," I said, meaning it as much as I had ever meant anything in my life. I was not angry at her exactly, or even at my father. How can you be angry with a man you don't know? But there was a heaviness to the day that hadn't been there before, and a hopelessness.

I walked into the street without seeing it really, aching for something I could not even name.

8.

A week passed, during which I expected other letters from Kensington. I envisioned my father changing his mind, trying to retrieve the letter he had sent to America. A stern postmaster would have rebuked him and sent him home where, half wild with regret, he would compose a more accommodating response. This notion was so real to me that I actually imagined the words he would use, how he would frame his apology (which I, after letting him wait many days before hearing from me, would graciously accept).

No letter came, however. After expecting the letter each afternoon, I finally gave up waiting for it. I never let the thought go; I forced it somewhere to the back of my mind. It wasn't, after all, as if I'd lost anything I ever really had — or anyone. It was simply a troublesome issue that had been resurrected for a while, just long enough to bring fresh pain to me and old pain to my mother. Besides, there were other things to talk about.

On Tuesday afternoon, the maid left a note saying that Mrs. Kay Purcell had called and invited Mrs. Strong and her daughter, Miss Blake, to dinner the following Friday evening. This was written in a sloping hand. Maria, mother's regular housekeeper, liked things formal. She was happiest when she got to "mister" and "miss" people at gallery openings.

Ironically, though my mother was her boss, Maria always got *her* title wrong. As far back as I can remember, Mother spurned the "Ms." or "Mrs." forms: she called herself *Miss* Strong, as a never-married woman would. When I asked her why, she said it was a matter of personal preference. People ought to be encouraged to have things as they liked.

I thought of this as I read the note and thought, too, of how I could convince my mother that we ought to go. It was clear that Mrs. Purcell was offering us dinner as a form of reciprocation, their food in return for our food, and that if my mother refused to go, there might be no further invitations. For some reason, it struck me as important for us to go to Jon's and have dinner on his terrain. My mother would have to be less haughty and arty in someone else's home. I wasn't sure why this was so, but I was fairly certain that it was. Perhaps over there she would behave like a normal mother and get to like Kay Purcell, maybe almost as much as I liked Jon.

At six, when she finally opened the front door,

I thrust the note under her nose, too wound up to wait.

"What's this?"

"An invitation." I drew back but inwardly bucked with impatience, an overeager kid.

She kicked off her shoes, moved to a chair, put on her reading glasses. Frowned.

"What's wrong?"

"Nothing," she said. "Make me some Perrier water and lime, sweetheart? I'm so tired I feel half dead."

I did as she asked, pouring the sparkling water into a good crystal goblet and slicing the lime paper-thin. If I did everything right, perhaps she would act pleased and agree to go to Jon's. That was in my mind as I handed her a linen napkin and the chilled Perrier, and began massaging her neck with my free hand.

"Hard day?" I said, kneading.

"No. An interesting one. A new acrylic came in that took my breath away. From your favorite artist and mine, old Alex."

I took my hands off her neck and sat down, facing her.

"What was it like?"

"Wonderful! Big. Blake, he's growing by leaps and bounds. I was amazed he hadn't shipped this one off to New York."

"Why didn't he?"

"He may yet, if we don't get his price. But, and this is the really exciting thing, he says the one he's just begun is even better! And do you know, I believe him. Alex never exaggerates. His use of color is getting to be absolutely . . ."

I held up a hand, tired of Alex Levine and his use of color.

"What?" she said, fighting irritation.

"You *are* going to say yes to Mrs. Purcell?"

She looked at me blankly, as if I were speaking Serbo-Croation.

"The dinner! Mrs. Purcell's invitation to dinner. Friday. We're definitely going, aren't we?"

"Oh, Blake . . ."

"*What?*"

She put down her glass and sighed. "You don't want to start a thing with them, do you?"

"What do you mean, 'a thing'?"

"You don't want to get too friendly with them, do you?"

"Why not? They're terrifically nice people."

"Sweetheart" — she picked up the glass; took another sip — "they're boring. Nice, I'll grant you. But I've already given them one whole evening, for Aunt Holly's sake. When you get to be my age, even one evening wasted is too much wasted time."

"You might give them a chance."

"I did. I fed them. You were there, you must remember that!" She blinked like an owl, bewildered. "What is this about? Why on earth are you so defensive about the Purcells?"

I had rarely stood up to my mother before, but now I did. "Did you ever think about how narrow your life has gotten? Who do you see, besides people you've known from the gallery?"

"I *like* those people."

"You like them to the exclusion of every other kind of people."

To her credit, my mother looked thoughtful. "Do I? Does it really seem that way to you?"

"You're awfully single-minded."

"Yes." She reached for a cigarette and nodded slowly. "You have a point. Absolutely. But *you*. Are you really missing anything because of this habit of mine?"

"I don't see what you mean."

"Of course you do. I mean, is there anything specific you're missing out on, because of the nature of my friendships? Is there any reason why you can't branch out on your own a bit, if you want to mix with different types?"

"I just want you to like the Purcells!"

"Because you like Jon so much."

"Well, yes. Of course that's one reason. And because I think, if you gave them a chance, you'd really enjoy them. Or people like them."

She nodded her head slowly. "I know the feeling. I've long thought, if your father would give you a chance, he'd find you irresistible. So why doesn't he? Can you tell me that? Why doesn't he, when it would be so sensible for him to?"

I was shocked by what I took to be her cruelty, until I looked carefully at her face. It was drawn tightly as a bowstring. Ravaged.

"It's not the same thing," I said.

"No. Not exactly."

"Look," I told her, "I just think you work too hard. I think if you had dinner with the Purcells, or anybody who didn't have something to do with art, it would relax you."

Mother smiled. "Have we ever talked about

why I work as hard as I do? Having the artists to dinner, doing overtime at the gallery?"

I shook my head no.

"It's because I love it so damned much." She reached over and squeezed my shoulder. "I have a great love affair with paintings. Each morning, when I go to the gallery, things seem new. After all these years — light will play on an oil just a bit differently from the day before, perhaps. Or someone will come in with an exquisite fiber-hanging to sell — something in shades so delicate you can't imagine how they've been mixed. So you ask. And you learn something completely new."

"I know all that . . ."

"But you don't understand what pleasure it gives me," she said quietly. "My life is art, not because I love living in such a disciplined way, but because it's fun. Work is *fun*. The people I surround myself with, the ones you feel make me narrow, understand. Most of them feel exactly the same. They're gifted, sensitive friends. And I love them. And" — her voice changed slightly — "although they are excellent people . . . and although they have a fine son I am glad for you to see . . . I have no real common meeting-ground with the Purcells. Being with people like them, my darling, *not* going to the gallery, is work."

I stood up and walked to the window. Outside the sun was plunging beneath the foothills. The air shimmered with color, the kind that odd, little Alex Levine could capture to perfection, lustrous pearl, shell pink, slashes of magenta.

"Would you go for me?" I finally said.

56

"Would you ask me to? Knowing how I really feel?"

"I guess not," I said. "It would be a bad night."

"It would."

"You could be nice, though! You could make it a good night."

"Are we talking about a good time?" my mother said, "or good acting? Quite a difference between those two things."

"I still don't think you're being fair," I told her, lulled by the beauty before me.

Mother stood up, crossed over, softly kissed my cheek.

"I know," she said. "I know. I know."

The compromise we reached was my mother's idea: on the night of the Purcell's proposed dinner, she would make her excuses but, if it was agreeable with Jon's parents, I would go.

Mrs. Purcell agreed with the plan so quickly that I wondered whether she was secretly relieved at not having to deal with both of us. In any event, I would get to see Jon's family in their home, which would appease the curiosity that had been building in me from the first night of our acquaintance.

The night of the dinner, my mother decided to have an impromptu party of her own. Kevin Marasco, a sculptor who was famous for his impressions of giant, abstract vegetables, had stopped in Santa Fe en route from San Francisco to Boston, where his *Cauliflower Planet* was being installed at Harvard. It weighed hundreds of tons and looked like a bronze meatball. My mother was so excited that she ordered a case of French champagne from Cliff's and got on the hotline to all of her friends.

"We have to help Kevin celebrate the placement of this monster," she said at least a dozen times, smoking and laughing into the phone. "Seriously, his *Cumcumber Galaxy* got a page in *Newsweek*, and it wasn't half as electrifying as the *Cauliflower*. . . ."

Guests had already begun to invade the house by the time I was ready to leave for the Purcells'. I planned to walk over there and have Jon drive me back, so he wouldn't have to mix it up with any of the stranger artists.

From the looks of things, they were going to be out in force. Antoinette Ludlow, a weaver, was there in her Armenian wedding dress. Antoinette had been coming into the gallery for five years, and I have never seen her wear anything but that dress, even though she is English, not Armenian, and to my knowledge has never been married. The only part of her uniform that varies is the footwear. In wintertime, she wears brown Dingo boots, and in hot weather, she switches to Famolare sandals.

Her date for the evening was Cosmo Gilbert, a portraitist who specializes in torsos. His studio is covered with torsos of friends and famous people. It's supposed to be "in" to have Cosmo paint your midriff, but I've never understood why. When he asked me to pose, I told him he would have to include my neck and shoulders, too. That seemed to kill his desire to work with me. He never brought it up again.

There were others toasting the white-haired Marasco with my mother's champagne: Loren Taborsky, a Czech watercolorist; Billie Fontayne, the owner of a competing gallery.

Mother herself was dressed all in Chinese red, except for her black cloth slippers from the UNICEF shop. She seemed fragile as an orchid, with her fine-boned hands waving a lighted Dunhill. So many people crowded around her that I didn't even try to wedge in for a good-bye.

I pulled my sweater on and headed out the door.

It took twenty minutes to walk over there. By the time I arrived, night had swept the neighborhood and lights were palely visible through the windows of the Purcells' Stamm house.

"Well, Blake," Mrs. Purcell said when I had rung the doorbell and been admitted inside, "this is great. Jon hasn't had company for dinner since we moved to Santa Fe. I miss cooking for his friends. If your mother had been able to come, I would have served drinks, but . . ." her voice trailed off. "Can I get you something nonalcoholic?"

I told her I wasn't very thirsty, but still she disappeared into the kitchen and came out with a chilled glass of grape juice. Jon was behind her, carrying another.

"Pepper shrimp for dinner," he said.

"Pepper and shrimp are two of my favorite things, but I've never had them together. Is it made like it sounds?"

"Exactly," Mrs. Purcell said. "Come on, I'll show you."

I followed her into the kitchen, which was a veritable page from *Bon Appetit,* with its spice racks and baskets extending from pine walls, its knives sunken in wooden blocks, and geraniums tumbling from the windows. It was the kitchen of a true cook who loves her work and takes it seriously.

There was a feeling in that room that is hard to describe — an almost palpable warmth and gentleness. The combination of good smells, bright, blended colors, and subdued but cheerful talk made me want to claim a corner for my own and move in there forever.

Mrs. Purcell and Jon joked with each other as they shelled the shrimp and placed them in a colander for rinsing. Mr. Purcell came home from work and kissed his wife. Television news droned softly in the background, Dan Rather dominating the soundwaves instead of the Luciano Pavarotti arias my mother always had on.

"Does your mother have an international cooker?" Mrs. Purcell asked me.

"I don't know. I don't think so."

"They're like woks, only flat-bottomed."

"She may," I said, "but I doubt if she knows how to use it. She doesn't like cooking much."

"It's the easiest pan in the kitchen to use. Nothing to it, Blake. Watch." She melted a stick of butter in the broad, copper pan, then tossed in the shrimp to sizzle. While she turned them onto their sides, Jon grated in fresh, black peppercorns, as if this were an old ritual and he knew his part by heart.

When the shrimp began to curl, Mrs. Purcell took a bottle of La You red oil ("I only bring it out for Szechuan dishes, and for this") and sprinkled a drop or two into the melted butter.

It smelled wonderful and tasted even better. The table had been set with bone china and crystal goblets; a small bowl of hothouse carnations brightened the room.

While we ate, the Purcells asked each other the questions I'd imagined married people asked. How was your day? Did you hear the news about . . . ? Was there anything in the mail for me? What do you want to do this Sunday, take a drive?

I knew my mother would have been fidgeting by now, but what bored her, comforted me. It was the most peaceful evening I could ever remember. No one chain-smoked, no one vaulted around the house looking for invoices, no eccentric geniuses wandered in, demanding money and patronage.

"Jon just loves this shrimp. Don't you, Jon?"

Chewing his seventeenth, Jon nodded silently. I could just imagine Mrs. Purcell telling him, years and years ago, *Don't put too much in your mouth dear*. My mother, on the other hand, called in the famous photographer Paul Lankford to immortalize my spinach-spitting stage. He caught me with spinach on my face, smeared over my bare stomach, in my hair, and blew me up to poster size. I understand I was in the gallery office that way for years, with a small caption beneath that said, "Study in Green."

When I was ten and she could no longer put off teaching me manners, Mother sent me to Camp Elliott Barker with a note pinned to my boating shorts: *Tame this child. I've been unable to.*

They did, too. But that's another story.

I felt very content that night, watching Jon eat and pretending that it was our house we were eating in, his and mine, and not his parents'. It was not as if I actually yearned for that to happen — not at that point. But I had begun to enjoy the feel of being half of a couple, and doing normal couple-things.

"This was great, Mom," Jon said. And it was: the food, the flowers, the mother-and-father-presiding-together.

For the first time, I began to think I knew how it would feel to be part of a regular family. And I knew, too, that it was something I wanted.

Something, in fact, I had ached for.

9.

"WAS it fun?" Mother asked the following day. We had both slept in, but she still seemed weary. She flipped through the "Weekend" section of *The New Mexican*, a cloud of cigarette smoke encircling her unbrushed hair.

"The dinner at Jon's house, you mean?"

"Yes."

"It was fun."

She sighed as if I had announced I'd come down with mononucleosis. "Everyone missed you here. Lots of people commented on your absence."

"Thanks. You were missed there."

"Yes, well, we discussed that already."

I looked at her.

"Did Kay Purcell make a good dinner?"

"A terrific one. Pepper shrimp."

"Figures," Mother said. "From scratch, I'll bet. With her own two hands." She massaged her temples as if she had a migraine. "Were there flowers on the table?"

"Carnations. How did you know?"

"That kind of woman always puts flowers on the table."

I poured some hot water into a cup; mixed in some cappucino powder and cream. Mother's behavior bewildered me. She's never at her best in the morning, but she doesn't usually begin throwing zingers around until later in the day.

"Marasco's bringing some friends back from Boston," she remarked.

"Maybe you can throw another party then."

Her eyes narrowed. "What would be the point?" she demanded. "Why should I spend money and energy on a party my own daughter won't attend, just because she's infatuated with some boy . . . and likes the way his mother cooks?"

I put down the spoon and stared at her, understanding everything.

"Are you *jealous?* Can you possibly be jealous of the time I spent with the Purcells?"

Embarrassed, she turned away. Her shoulders were held like twin fortresses, high and still.

"It's difficult for me to understand how you can conceive of such a thing," she said dryly. "Would I trade places with someone like Kay Purcell? I think she put a hallucinogen in your shrimp last night, if you can even say that."

"Say what? It's nice over there. Really, you ought to see."

"Nice," she snorted, "is one of the most overrated words in the English language. *Nice* people put me to sleep."

We glared at each other for the space of a long minute. Then Mother began to laugh, aware of how ludicrous she had sounded. She shook her head and grinned a surrender.

"I'm sorry."

"No," I said.

"It's time you met a housewife or two. They used to be real American fixtures, like the sixty-watt light bulb." With that, she unfolded her long legs and crossed to the kitchen telephone. She punched out the gallery's number and began asking questions of her assistant. Had people commented on the new Levine? Was there mail about the small Marasco bronze? Anything interesting from United Parcel?

"I know that it's my morning off, but I'll be glad to come in if you think . . . or if you just want . . . all you have to do is tell me. . . . No? You're absolutely sure?"

At loose ends, she hung up the phone and walked outside.

I think I was actually obsessed by Jon, for a while.

There is a phrase, really a cliché, that states, "He was always in my thoughts." I doubt if the first person who ever said that meant, literally, always. Yet in my case, it was true. I saw Jon's face in dreams, I stopped reading in mid-sentence and conjured up the way his hand felt clasped in mine. Absentmindedly, I began calling other boys "Jon," and enjoying their double-take reactions, when I realized what I'd done.

When we were apart, I felt less alive. Wasn't

his place right next to mine? Weren't we better together than not? Didn't he want to be with me as much as I wanted to be with him?

He quickly became the most important person in the world to me. I cared about his problems even more than my own, but interestingly, we both had fewer after we started spending time together. He no longer spoke of Fort Lauderdale and his old friends. He began to make new ones.

Most of our evenings were spent at his house. I am trying to remember what we did there, but it's hard. Monopoly with friends, *Masterpiece Theater* on television . . . none of it mattered as much as being able to look sideways and see him stealing glances at me.

He had become bolder at kissing by then, and when our eyes met, he would reach for me and we would hold each other, until a footstep, a parent's cough, or the ring of a telephone stopped us. At those times, the physical separation was gentle enough.

But I had a feeling of outrage at those interruptions; the feeling of being torn.

10.

I HAVE always listened to girls discussing the parents of their boyfriends with an odd detachment.

"I don't think they like me. They look at me as if I were a snake or something."

"Oh, they're darling. And they think *I'm* darling . . ." (And I am, too.)

Usually, Darling-Whoever-She-Was would go on from there: "They bought me a present on my birthday. An aquamarine necklace. This thing I have on, isn't it beautiful? And my very own parents just wrote me a check! They're so unfeeling, and Bob's folks [or Ted's, or Harry's, or Andrew's] are the most feeling people in the whole wide world."

As I said, I used to listen to these diatribes with detachment, sometimes even nausea.

Yesterday, I heard myself confide, "Mrs. Purcell is the *greatest cook*. Mr. Purcell is the *nicest man*." (They're so feeling. My own mother is so unfeeling. All she thinks about is art.)

I had joined the club.

Mrs. Purcell liked to do embroidery in the evenings. She had cut pieces of Irish linen and skeins of vari-colored thread. Fitting the cloth into a tight, wooden embroidery hoop, she would sit beneath a bright swag lamp and stitch with total absorption. Her fingers flew over the imprinted designs, brightening them with red or blue or kelly green, stitching slogans: *Home Sweet Home*; *Forgiveness Is the Sweetener of Our Days.*

"Isn't this turning out pretty?" she would say. "Do you think I ought to make the flowers red, like poppies, or lavender, like violets? I can't decide which would look the best."

At first, I couldn't believe she really wanted my opinion. I was used to artists, after all: "You think the background should be brighter? What do you know? Nothing! If you knew anything, you would be the one holding the brush, not the one selling the pictures!"

But there Jon's mother sat, looking to me for a decision.

"Red would be nice," I said in a very tentative voice. "Unless, of course, you'd rather the lavender."

"Red it is." Brusquely. Then she would squint into the light, holding her needle in a steady right hand, trying to poke the thread through its eye. "Jon, make us all some tea, won't you? Not the store kind, either — the do-it-yourself kind. I have lemon grass and rose hips in the canister by the telephone book. Take three parts of lemon grass and the rest rose hips. Oh, Blake, he'll make a mess, go help him out, won't you? And use the good china. What are we saving it for anyway, a funeral?"

So we would be alone for awhile, bumping elbows in the kitchen, laughing, and brewing the tea. Sometimes he turned the radio to an AM station, flooding the house with music. My mother would have killed me if I'd done the same, but Mrs. Purcell rarely said anything more threatening than, "Turn it down a little, won't you? No, go ahead and listen. I didn't say turn it *off*, just a little lower will be fine."

"Just a little less cacaphony, son," Mr. Purcell would say in agreement.

Then the tea would be ready, Jon would lay a fire, the four of us would visit contentedly until it was time for me to go home.

When I arrived there, Mother would grunt a hello from the big Scandinavian dining table that doubled as her desk. Usually she wore bifocals and a Hermes scarf that tucked her hair into an efficient, slicked-back style. Chamber music always played in the background. The Espresso machine was always on.

I would move over to kiss her, sometimes having to dodge the pencils she tucked behind each ear, or the ignited Dunhill that hung from her determined lip.

"Good time?" she would ask.

"Yes."

"Quiche in the freezer, if you want to microwave a slice."

"Thank you. I ate with the Purcells."

Only then would her face ease into a composed mask, as if she were consciously weighing her alternatives and deciding to say nothing. Often, she would go right back to work, pretending busyness with pamphlets, lay-outs, promotional material, invitations.

All of it could have waited a day or more, so that we could visit, but she seemed not to need my company then. She began to pull into herself like a tortoise who has spied an enemy and knows it cannot run. It can only hope to seem insignificant, not worth catching and hurting at all.

If she had been a child, it would have looked as if she were pouting about something. And indeed she was: the more I saw of Jon, the fonder I grew of his family, the more acerbic she became.

These days, when she spoke of him at all, she conveniently "forgot" his name. He was That Boy, and his mother and father were Those People. (When she was in a particularly foul mood, their home became That House: "You're not going to That House again tonight? Aren't Those People going to feel you're wearing out your welcome?")

I tried to confront her with this, but she was always rushing out to an opening or dragging in from work, too keyed up or exhausted to listen to me.

A good picture of my mother at that time could have come from a medical journal. She was like the ladies in the tranquilizer ads, preoccupied, tense, running on coffee, cigarettes, and raw nerves.

70

For years, she had seemed bigger than life to me, but now most of the life had gone out of her. I had never before understood how much she depended on my always being home, waiting around to applaud her efforts. Since I had begun to outgrow that role, her displeasure knew no bounds. She still had me, but the me she really wanted was the year-ago version: her mild-mannered little girl.

There was a poem of Robert Louis Stevenson's she used to read to me when I was small:

> I have a little shadow
> That goes in and out with me.

In a not-unkind voice she used to tease, "That's you, Blake, my little shadow. What would Mother ever do without her little tag-along shadow, hmm?"

I had never had the courage to remonstrate: *"I don't want to be your shadow."* But I didn't. There was something about the idea that made me angry; something that made me feel less than a human being.

She was an exciting woman who cast a giant light wherever she went, but I was determined to be more than the shade she left behind.

And somehow Jon and my right to be with him, to blend into his family and their normal life, was all tied up in this other thing. I was going to love him if I wanted to. (I was going to show her.)

11.

THERE was a brochure on my desk when I walked into the room: *Camp Brendan, A Camp for the Arts, Rochester, New York.* There were pictures of teenagers painting oils, working pottery wheels, making charcoal sketches. All of of them were smiling as if a rich uncle had just died and left them a bundle. The Camp Brendan public relations officer sure knew his stuff.

On top of the brochure was a note:

Sweetheart,
Don't these kids look happy? Had you forgotten that this is the year you'll be old enough to attend Brendan? Did you know that my old friend Maxie Baehr is teaching a junior course in art administration there? Don't you want to get busy and fill out the application?

Love,
Mom

I groaned and looked through the brochure. It was wonderful. It cost a fortune to get in, dozens of famous artists were going to teach courses there, and there would be two excursions into New York City to see shows, eat at restaurants, and browse through private studios that were never (of course) open to the public. My mother had been planning to send me to Brendan for years. She had gone when she was a teenager, and still spoke of it as if it were the high point of her life.

But the course was ten weeks long. How could I leave Jon for ten weeks? That was seventy days. One thousand six hundred eighty hours. A lifetime.

My mother must have known that I would think of that. Every word in her note was part of a question, as if she no longer felt she could just tell me something and have my understanding.

I collapsed on the bed and finished reading every word of the brochure. Some things had been underlined: Maxie Baehr's name and Andy Warhol's had been underscored repeatedly.

Outside, a robin redbreast brushed against my window. His eye was a black O, staring at me as if he were my mother demanding a decision.

"I don't know," I foolishly said to the bird.

Disinterested, it flew away.

"Maybe Jon could go, too." But I was talking to an empty window now, my voice less than a whisper in the thickening dark.

That night as I tried to sleep, I was assaulted by questions. If I had to choose between camp

74

and Jon, which would I choose? If I had to choose
between Jon and art?

Did you forget this is the year you'll be old
enough to attend Brendan?

An image of my mother's face broke through
my closed eyelids, determined, yet pleading.
Are you going to that boy's house again?

I woke up in a sweat, thinking it was the middle
of the night. But my alarm clock was buzzing,
and sun was spilling through an eastern window.

On the floor, the Brendan brochure with its
smiling artists lay crumpled in a ball. I must have
thrown it there during a dream, I thought. But I
had no memory of doing anything like that.

Feeling disoriented, I turned off the alarm clock
and headed for the kitchen. My mother was already there, sipping peach nectar from a Water-
ford glass. She was dressed all in black, except for
a red ascot at her throat, much like the robin of
the night before. One black boot swung in front
of another; red bracelets slashed the pale skin of
her wrists.

"Sleep well?" she said.

"Fine."

"That's good," she said. "Me, too."

"I found the brochure."

"And?" she said.

"And ten weeks is an awfully long time to be
away from here. We've never been apart that
long."

Her face softened. "No," she agreed. "We

haven't." I could tell that she was remembering that the two of us had always been together, from the time I was a baby. Just her and me. Then her expression changed. "Are you certain it's not Jon you'll be missing?"

"Well, sure. Him, too."

"Blake, you have to have some time away from that boy. He's a very nice boy, I'll grant you that, but you're much too young to be serious about anyone."

"Don't worry," I said, "okay? We're not talking about eloping or anything."

"You spend far too much time alone with him."

"What do you mean by that?"

She flushed. "I just mean it's not a good idea for two young, healthy people who are attracted to each other to spend as much time together as you do. It's inviting trouble."

I felt sick to my stomach. Obviously, she was talking about sex. That was perfectly clear, the way she avoided my eyes and used that dumb euphemism "trouble" instead of a real word. And she wasn't about to let up, either; she kept digging a deeper and deeper hole for herself.

"We don't need to talk about anything, do we?" she said.

I felt torn between two emotions. I wanted to bash her, on the one hand, and on the other hand, I felt sorry for her. She had such a reputation for being liberal and broad-minded about people's personal lives, largely because artists have such messy ones. Some artists, anyway. Then the minute her own daughter gets a boyfriend, she goes nuts, wondering what they do when she's not around. Before she could give me any more of the third degree, I mumbled, "We're not doing anything, okay? Like you mean. Not *anything!*"

"Well," she said in this embarrassed, relieved voice, "if you're sure."

"No, I'm not sure," I shouted. "I'm too dumb to know what I'm talking about! You know everything and I don't know anything!"

"Blake," my mother said, all agitated. Her getting-ready-to-apologize voice, is what it was.

But I wasn't going to wait around for that. I'd heard enough. While she was babbling that she was sorry, she'd misjudged good old Jon and good old me, I picked up a glass of juice and went back to my room.

Once I was there, I really let the door slam. The juice danced in its glass and the walls shook.

It felt so good I wished there were a reason to slam it again.

12.

THE MAJOR INSPIRATION OF MY TEENAGED LIFE

Write a 200-word theme on "The Major Inspiration of My Teenaged Life." You may choose one of the following: A Sports Star, A Politician, A Good Teacher You Have Had in the Past (or This Year), A Relative, A Best Friend, A Person of Your Own Choice. Staple Your Rough Draft to Your Final Draft and Hand It in After One Hour. Do Not Talk to Me, I Am Grading. Jon Purcell, Go to the Principal's Office and Call Your Mother.

It took me two minutes to read the whole note on Miss Nadia Delancey's blackboard, and another thirty seconds to make sure that Jon was gone.

He was. He'd left his backpack with the *Fort Lauderdale Loves Tourists* emblem on top of his desk. A Butterfinger bar peeked out of its open corner. I sneaked it out and put it in my purse to give back to him later. People were always stealing each other's food in Miss Delancey's class. It was sort of a standing joke. The unfunny part was that you never got it back. When it was gone, it was gone forever. If Jon had been in Santa Fe longer, he would have been smarter about protective measures. I knew three people who stashed plastic-wrapped raisins in their shoes.

I was thinking about that, wondering how they walked straight with dried fruit squishing beneath their toes, and what a raisin would taste like with toe smell all over it, when Jon walked into the room. He shot me a very peculiar look, almost a hostile one, and slipped into his chair.

I wrote a note and handed it over:

What on earth is wrong? You look like you just lost your best friend!!!

He wadded the note up and started scribbling one of his own. In another minute I was reading:

Your mother did the weirdest thing! She called up my mother and said the only reason you weren't excited about going to Art Camp was because you didn't want to leave me. She also said would it be possible for my mother to keep me away from you in the future. She said, not entirely, but at least 50% of the time!!! Blake, what is going on? Is your mother crazy or what? *Also*, this is the weirdest part of all, after she said all that stuff, *then* she invited me to your birthday dinner! She also invited my parents!

She said that we were your favorite friends in Santa Fe, after all that neurotic keep-them-away-from-each-other junk.

Would you please tell me what is going on???

Write your theme first though. I heard this was a fourth of our term grade, if you can believe it.

I love you forever!
Jon
Love—Kisses—Hugs—XXX
(This whole thing is really strange & odd!!)

I had to agree. In fact, I got so mad reading Jon's note that all I could think about was how good it would feel to scream at my mother. I planned exactly which words I would use, all her least favorite ones heading the list. Then I planned how I was going to tell her there was no way I would go to her stupid old Brendan, not after what she'd done. I'd never been so embarrassed in my life, and I've been embarrassed plenty.

Because I couldn't get my mind off my mother, how mad I felt at her, I decided to make her "THE MAJOR INSPIRATION OF MY TEEN-AGED LIFE." She absolutely was that, and this way I wouldn't have to make my brain, which is essentially a one-track one, zigzag back and forth. I took out a Bic FlairTip, chewed on the end of it for about three minutes, and began to write:

The Major Inspiration of My
Teenaged Life
The major inspiration of my teenaged life
would be my mother, Lois Strong. I think

it's funny that her name is Strong, because she is the strongest woman I know. If you do something she doesn't think you should, or if you live your life differently from hers, watch out! She runs an art gallery, which you probably already know. Everyone knows about the gallery and everyone knows about her. I guess she's a little bit famous. In fact, in Santa Fe, she's famous quite a lot. Almost all of her friends are famous, too. Andy Warhol, Georgia O'Keeffe. I'll bet Rembrandt would be coming to her cocktail parties and openings, except he's dead. If he were alive, though, he'd be my mother's friend. She'd get all gushy and excited and kiss him on the cheek and call him by his first name, which escapes me for the moment. But you can bet my mother would know. That's the way she is, all first-namey and ultra-friendly with artists and all cold and calculating with the rest of the world.

Right now she wants me to go to Brendan Art Camp, to get me away from a very satisfying personal life that I have put together. But since it's not the sort of life she wants me to have, off I go! I'm not saying I hate her because in a funny way I do love her. But I just wish she'd back off sometimes, and let me enjoy myself and make my own mistakes!

It's very hard to be the daughter of a well-known and successful mother. It makes you think, well, what if that doesn't happen to me? Will I be worthless? Will she be ashamed of me instead of proud? I know it shouldn't matter how she feels. I should be mature enough to value my own opinion more. She is "the major inspiration of my teenaged life." But not always 100% in a good way: Today she did something that made me so mad I'm sick to my stomach. I can't believe she would do this particular thing, but she did. She dislikes a boy who I care for very, very much — not because he's bad or dumb, but because she's afraid I'll love him so much I won't "develop" myself. My mind, I believe she means. And I have told her that I would, and she just won't listen!

Just because she's been disappointed in men, does that mean I automatically will be, too? No! But try to tell her that.

There are some good things, too, but right now it's just so hard to think of any. I can do that better later. Maybe someday you will ask us to write a theme about whether we still feel the same about "the major inspirations of our teenaged lives," and if so, maybe I can say something nicer then.

P.S. I know it's not right to put a P.S. on a theme, but when it comes time to read these aloud, it would be good if you did not call on me, I think.

13.

THE morning of my sixteenth birthday, I lay in bed and felt sad. In Santa Fe, the truly big birthday for girls is fifteen. Hispanic families call their fifteen-year-old daughters "quinceaneras," and the really old-line families give special parties called Las Quinceaneras to mark the day. My mother is as Anglo as they come, but she loves the Hispanic culture so much that she gave me a similar kind of party last year. She is always saying that she really wishes she were Hispanic, or Jewish, or Chinese, or Indian. The more exotic the race, the more she wants to belong to it.

She must have the feeling that being an Anglo-American is boring and run-of-the-mill. Some people are born wanting to be what they aren't, and I guess my mother is just one of those. If she had been born a Navajo princess, she would probably be upset because she couldn't be an Anglo art dealer in Santa Fe. Tough, is the way I feel about that. She should just appreciate being alive and quit wanting to change everything around different ways.

I was lying on my stomach thinking about that, about how I wished she'd straighten up and be a regular mother and stay out of my business, when she knocked on the door and came in with some Swiss hot chocolate.

"A sweet for my sweet sixteen."

My stomach turned over. "No thanks," I said.

"It's *imported*. This isn't Nestlés, it's something I made from scratch, for you, with my own hands, Blake!"

"Okay," I said. I drank the chocolate, which tasted like chocolate, not Switzerland. The only difference is that it was just a little bit flatter, as if it had hung around in a tin can for months and months on some pier. I'll bet she paid triple for it, too.

"My big girl," she said.

I stared at my toes and tried to keep my mouth shut.

"Such a beautiful, big girl I have . . ."

"Are you going to behave yourself tonight with the Purcells?" I asked. The minute it was out of my mouth, I felt like groaning. That was the sort of question that my mother thought was "fresh." She wouldn't hit me for it, or yell at me, but she'd make her eyes all defeated-looking, as if she'd spent the best years of her life bringing me up, only to fail. I hate stuff like that.

"*Behave* myself?" The sad business with the eyes was already underway.

"Look, all I meant was, I know they're not as

86

much fun for you as they are for me. Just use your good manners with them, okay? Don't treat them like they're . . ."

"What?" she said, bewildered.

"Just don't treat them like they're beneath you, or something. They're not."

She picked up the empty chocolate cup and kissed me as if she were a saint being charitable to some leper. "It's your birthday. We'll do this your way." Then she padded out of the room, probably to let me get the nastiness out of my system. Sometimes I wish she would fight me instead of being placid and walking away, but walking away is what she generally does.

By the time I made it to the kitchen to get breakfast, she had already gone. A small package wrapped in chocolate brown paper with slender gold ties sat by my cereal bowl. Underneath it was a birthday card.

The front of the card was a copy of one of Picasso's nudes, which sounds worse than it is. With Picasso, it's hard to say what's naked and what isn't. I didn't recognize one single part of male or female anatomy, just a montage of what looked like pieces from an alarm clock. But the title said "Nude," so that must be what it was.

Inside the box lay a necklace that was copied from the Elizabethan period. I knew that, because there was a white card enclosed: NECKLACE COPIED FROM THE ELIZABETHAN PERIOD, MUSEUM OF ANTIQUARIAN ART.

Art, art, art. What I really wanted was records for my stereo.

I picked up a box of Shredded Wheat and slammed it down on the table again, not too thrilled with the idea of breakfast. I would be eating a big birthday dinner later on, maybe Gruyère Veal at Cousart's, which was my favorite. That is, if I could choke any of it down. I thought about how it would be that night, The Incredible Lois Strong versus The Purcells. Then I stuffed the Elizabethan necklace back into its airy little box and headed out the door.

Later in the day, "The Major Inspiration of My Teenaged Life" was handed back to me. I made B—, because I started a sentence with a preposition and did lousy on my paragraphing. For content, I made A—. Miss Nadia Delancey had taken a violet marker and written over my essay:

This took courage to write! Many people do not get along well with their mothers, but how many of us can express those feelings? Sometimes I do not get along well with my own mother. She lives in Des Moines and thinks she's great. President of the Garden Club, Symphony Guild — she's that kind of mother. So I know how you feel! She is always after me to change my ways, to get a better job than teaching, to get married, to get a haircut, or wear a different kind of makeup. So you see, these problems never stop. When I got my master's degree, did she even care? No — she was upset that I didn't have a husband yet. I hope that you and the boy in your "personal life" find happiness

despite your Mother Problems. Don't tell
anyone else, but because of my mother I am
still in therapy. It costs $45 an hour but I
am afraid to quit, because my mother
messed me up so badly! Sincerely, your
teacher, Nadia Delancey

I know that Miss Delancey wrote that to make
me feel better, because she kept giving me little
smiles all through class. If anything, though, it
made me feel worse. The idea that I would still
be my mother's shadow ten or fifteen years down
the road almost put me away.

Another thing: I wasn't all that thrilled about
knowing Miss Nadia Delancey's personal secrets.
What business was it of mine, that she was in
therapy because her mother was such hot stuff?
From then on, I knew I would look at her and
think of her stretched out on some analyst's
couch, whining about her mother. As far as I was
concerned, her mother was right about one thing,
the makeup: Miss Delancey pasted on these
spider-leg, artificial eyelashes every single morning. They really looked as if two black widows
were hitchhiking on her irises. They cheapened
her entire appearance, which wasn't that expensive to begin with.

I was so depressed that it felt like my hun-
dredth birthday instead of my sixteenth, until Jon
took my arm in the hall and slipped some paper
into my free hand.

"Don't read it until later," he said. Then he disappeared.

People should never tell me to read something

later; I can't stand the suspense. Right in the middle of the hall, I unfolded the paper and began to read:

"BLAKE CANNABERRY:
THE MAJOR INSPIRATION
OF MY TEENAGED LIFE"

Form: A —
Content: A —

Only once in a lifetime do you meet someone who is so perfectly attuned to your own spirit. Blake Cannaberry is such a friend. She knows what I am going to say before I open my mouth. She enjoys the same things I enjoy. She wants to live the same kind of exciting life I want to live.

When I talk to Blake about important things, I forget that I am young. I feel like a man of my father's age, because she listens to my opinions and gives me excellent advice from her own head.

It is hard to discuss how I feel about Blake, because that is really PRIVATE!!! [*Jon — three exclamation points are two too many, if you know what I mean. Miss N.D.*] Suffice it to say that I find her a wonderful young lady. She is not just pretty, she is also intelligent. She comes from a different sort of home. Her parents are divorced, you know. And sometimes I wonder about that. I fear that she may be unstable and want to divorce also, when she is older. On the other hand, perhaps this tragedy has taught her the real value of an American family.

I stopped reading then.

It was wonderful that Jon had written about me. On the other hand, some of the things he said seemed really peculiar. I had never thought of my mother's divorce as a tragedy, only a nuisance on occasions like Father's Day. She was happy the way she was. And although we fought sometimes, I think she was happy that we were together.

It seemed odd that Jon would run on and on about the "value of the American family," when I felt that I had a perfectly fine American family myself. My mother and I were just two people, but we were relatives. We lived together. She took care of me, when she wasn't busy trying to make me crazy, or trying to make deals with crazy artists.

For the very first time, I began to get a glimmer of what my mother had meant when she said the Purcells weren't her kind of people. Before, it seemed that they had everything and we had nothing. I remembered dinners at their house, Mr. Purcell with his slippers and his television programs, Mrs. Purcell with her African violets and pepper shrimp. Maybe they talked about us when I wasn't around: *"Poor Blake, no father and a mother that's always so busy."*

My stomach began to feel a little sour. But at that point, I couldn't have explained why. I guess I felt it wasn't in my best interests to understand.

Cousart's is in a quiet part of downtown Santa Fe. Very few tourists go there, because it's off the beaten path. I always check the license plates to see how many tourists, how many Santa Feans. The night of my birthday dinner every car there had New Mexico plates, except for the Purcells'. They were still carting around their Florida license and a Fort Lauderdale beach decal that said: FUN IN THE SUN!

The restaurant looks more like a house than a place of business. It's very airy and neat-looking, and makes you think that you're eating with someone's Aunt Martha, instead of paying for your food.

"Hel-*lo* there," my mother said when she saw the Purcells. They were already seated at a table for five. Mr. Purcell wore a polyester suit and Mrs. Purcell wore an expression that said she was going to be polite to my mother even if she popped a nerve doing it.

"Hello," Mrs. Purcell answered. She smiled like a cat in the dark.

I sat by Jon, who was behaving just like himself, and we began to read our menus.

"Can we have anything we want?" I asked.

"You know it," my mother said. "A sixteenth birthday is very special."

I began to look at the choices. There was Gruyère Veal, all right, but it was the most expensive thing on the menu. I hadn't remembered that. Maybe if I ordered it, everybody else would, and then my mother would have to pay an entire fortune just to settle the dinner check. I checked out the lasagne and the trout.

"Are you ready to order?" the waitress asked.

Mother told her no, to wait a minute. In about another five or six minutes, she came again, and everyone started to order. Mr. and Mrs. Purcell ordered the trout special, and mother ordered chicken breasts in champagne. I got chicken breasts, too, and Jon ordered Steak Tartare.

"Are you sure you want that?" my mother said, a strange smile on her face.

"Yes, ma'am," Jon said. "Medium well, please."

The waitress gave him a condescending look and said, "Steak Tartare is raw meat. That's what it *is*. It's never cooked. At Cousart's, it's served with a raw egg on top."

Jon got very pink and looked sick. "Can you cook it this time?" he said.

The waitress shook her head no. "Chef won't do it. I've asked him before, young man. Chef gets very upset when I ask him that. Try the chicken breasts, if you want something cooked."

He coughed as if he had swallowed the wrong way. "I'll have the chicken breasts, then," he said, handing over the menu.

"Well," my mother said. "That's that."

She looked incredibly pretty, with a copper-colored suit and gold earrings on. It wasn't an arty suit at all. It was something she could have worn into banks and grocery stores.

"Happy birthday, Blake," Jon said. He gave me a very small box he'd been hiding. "I hope this fits."

I opened it up and gasped. Inside was a small, gold friendship ring, with our initials engraved on the top: BC—JP.

"Do you like it?"

"I love it!"

"Does it fit?"

I pulled it out of the box and tried it on. It fit as if he had measured my finger, which he hadn't. I twisted it around and around, trying to see the initials glint in the subdued light.

"What does it mean?" my mother said dryly.

"Just friendship," Mrs. Purcell quickly said.

I extended my hand to give my mother a better look.

"Friendship is all it means," Mrs. Purcell emphasized.

My mother pushed her plate away. "So you said."

After dinner, the waitress brought in a cake and everyone sang "Happy Birthday." After a certain point in life, that is embarrassing, and I squirmed until they were through.

While the cake was being passed, Mr. Purcell asked my mother, "What was your gift to Blake this year?"

"Well, the dinner."

"And a necklace," I said. "An Elizabethan one."

"What's that?"

"It's a necklace crafted the way they were in Elizabethan days," I said.

"Oh. That's what I thought it was, too."

Mother straightened in her chair and dabbed her lips with a linen napkin. "I'm giving Blake one more surprise," she said.

A soft chorus of *Whats?* slithered around the table.

She opened her purse and pulled out a flat envelope. "Take a look," she said.

I tested its flap and found that it was gummed.

Using a dinner knife as a letter opener, I extracted a piece of thin, yellow paper and tried to make out its print in the poor light.

"It's your receipt for Brendan Art Camp," Mother said, unable to wait for my deciphering. "All paid up. You'll leave in June."

"How nice," Mrs. Purcell said in a loud voice. But Jon looked on with a stricken face, and Mr. Purcell seemed puzzled.

"You're going in June?" Jon said. "How long will you be gone? *Blake?* Did you know she was going to send you away in June?"

"Not for sure, I didn't. I thought we were going to talk about it before a final decision was made."

It was my mother's turn to look uneasy. "Well, we *were,*" she said behind a cloud of cigarette smoke. "But the places were filling up fast, and I knew that deep inside, Blake wanted to go. A summer seems like a long time, but it isn't, you know. And this is an experience she'll remember all her life."

My face began to tingle, as if nerve endings were sprouting on top of my epidermis. People continued to talk, but they sounded far away and used indistinct words. I sat with the yellow paper in my hand and wondered how it would feel to touch it to the lighted candle and watch it curl into an ash.

Is anything wrong? Mouths were moving, they were saying those three words, but I was too upset to comprehend which mouths, or to wonder about polite ways to respond.

"You just want to get me away from Jon," I said instead.

95

All talk stopped.

"You want me away from Jon," I repeated in a louder voice. "You're afraid if I stay here, with him, I'll be normal and happy. Not like you. Not like your friends. And you know what? You're *right* to be afraid. Because that's exactly what would happen to me if I stayed in Santa Fe with Jon. I'd be happy. And we can't have that, can we? Not for a woman from our family. We don't go in for simple happiness, do we, when we can have artistic anguish or workamania instead?"

"Blake — " my mother started to say.

"We can't have that, can we?"

I think I really wanted her to stay and fight with me; to explain. I didn't care if the Purcells heard what we said and were embarrassed by it. It was time to call her on this. There would never be a better time.

"Isn't that right?"

But she seemed not to hear me. She threw some money on the table and drew on her coat. "Please forgive me," she said. "No, please, stay. Please. That's better. Just stay."

Then she was flying out the door without a glance at me, or at any of us. The light from the candle flickered at the cold, onrushing air, then stabilized and grew bright again as the door swung firmly shut.

When I am wrong I am quick to apologize, but I did not feel particularly wrong that night. The look on my mother's face convinced me that there was truth in what I had said. So I finished my dinner, determinedly apologetic and upbeat. We were like a World War II film set in England.

"Sorry chaps, but these things happen, and what is there but to make the best of it?"

It worked well, but not well enough to save the evening. As soon as they could, Mr. and Mrs. Purcell left saying how much they hoped everything would be all right, and surely it would be, and if it *weren't,* why then, they would be right there to "talk to." So Jon and I were alone, and the waitress was beginning to get aggressive about clearing the table of china and of us.

"A movie?" Jon suggested.

We got a newspaper outside and looked through the entertainment page. There was nothing good, and of the bad there was nothing fun.

"We could just take a walk," I said.

"Are you up to that?"

The chicken settled heavily in my stomach, its champagne undertones making me faintly nauseous. "What else is there?"

"We could go to my house."

"I think your parents wanted to be rid of us."

"We could go to your house, then."

"Sure we could," I said.

"Look, Blake, could you be wrong about this? Could it just be a present instead of a punishment?"

"Half and half, maybe."

"What could she be punishing you *for*? It's just not sensible."

"She's punishing me for not being her," I said. As soon as it was out of my mouth, I knew that it was true. All she had ever wanted from me was to make Blake Cannaberry into a junior grade

Lois Strong. She was her idea of success, after all.

We walked down Alameda and turned on Old Santa Fe Trail, passing delicious-smelling restaurants and prosperous-looking tourists. Two nuns crossed in front of us, their short skirts exposing woolen socks and worn shoes. Their faces were closed, and I wondered how it would be to swear a vow of poverty and never eat a dinner like the one I had just eaten at Cousart's; never to hang expensive art on a wall. It seemed romantic and yet not. I had an idea that after awhile it would just make me tired and sad to be that poor, even if it were part of a noble vocation.

My mother had told me that we were poor once. She told anecdotes about it and made it sound almost fun, scraping to keep alive in big New York City. With a stab, I wondered if it had been fun, really, or if she had just made up a scenario she thought I would like.

"What are you thinking about?" Jon said.

"Nothing."

"Yes, you were."

"Those Catholic sisters," I said then.

"What about them?"

They disappeared in De Vargas Alley, their dark skirts fading to shadow. "I was really thinking about my mother," I said.

"She tried to give you a nice birthday, I think. I really do think that," Jon said.

"I know."

"The dinner and everything. It was nice."

"They always are — my birthdays. Every year she thinks up special things. We've never done the same thing twice."

"Maybe you should make up with her, Blake."

"I don't have anything to apologize for."

"I didn't say that you did," Jon told me. "I just said maybe you should make up with her. That's all."

"Oh, Jon."

"Oh, Blake." He mimicked my voice perfectly, and I turned to get him, but he started to run. Even in his street shoes, he was fast. Just as I was running out of breath, really hurting, he made a quick turn onto a side street and stopped in front of my mother's gallery.

"Look. There are lights on," he said when I caught up with him.

I wheezed in reply.

"She's in there, Blake. See? Don't you think you ought to go see her?"

"If you come with me," I said.

"No."

"Why not?"

"We can't do everything together. This is something you ought to do alone."

"Would you wait for me if I did?"

"Right here," he promised. "Right within sight."

"I won't be five minutes," I said.

"Take all the time you want. I'm tired, anyway. You go in there and talk to your mother. I'll rest while you do."

I let him squeeze my arm, which was supposed to show affection, I guess, but it seemed to me for a moment that he was exerting pressure to make sure I complied. Still, I took a deep breath, then another, and walked in.

She had her back turned, but she must have

recognized my walk (or my voice — had we been loud outside?), for she said, "Hello, Blake," without checking to make sure that it was me.

"Mother — " My own voice was thin and defensive.

"Did you finish your dinner?"

"Yes."

"Was it good?"

"Yes. I didn't get to tell you it was good. But it was."

"I thought so, too. I'm glad you liked it. Cousart's is wonderful."

"It is."

"It really is. Really."

I sat down and thought how crazy it was, that kind of small talk, after such an ugly scene. We wore politeness like jewelry — conspicuously, showily.

"You're through with the evening early," she said.

"Not quite. Jon's still outside."

"Is he?" She seemed confused by that, and turned to look at the window. "I can't see him. Where is he?"

"Out there someplace. I guess he went around the corner."

"Well, don't you want to invite him in? Isn't it cold out there?"

"He didn't want to come."

"Oh, well. In that case."

I broke first. "Look," I said. "About tonight. It was awful. I feel *awful* about it."

"Well," she said, making a weak smile, "that's two of us. What happened?"

100

"I don't know. Just what I told you."

"You really think I'm trying to get you away from Jon?"

"I don't know." I allowed myself a sigh. "I just don't know."

"Well, I'm not," my mother said. She turned away from me then and walked over to the north wall of her gallery. "Do you like this lithograph?" she asked me. "It's new. I like it very much, I think. It catches the light different ways. Do you see what I mean?" She went over to the dimmer and adjusted the glare. "There, do you see? It seems more pastel now. Don't you think it seems more pastel?"

"A little more pastel."

"I think so, too." She turned the lights back up and gave me an odd look. "Do you know, you'll be eighteen before we know it? Eighteen, Blake! Old enough to do whatever you please. Marry this Jon Purcell, or whatever young people do these days when they want to be together. He's the marrying sort, I'd guess. From that family. So you'll be gone, and I know it. Don't think that I don't. Mothers and daughters don't stick together."

"Come on. Of course they do."

"No." She seemed intent on refuting me. "*No*. These are what I'll have forever. These. Not you."

"What?" But even as I asked, I knew. She was talking about her pictures.

"We have quite a collection, you know," she was telling me. "Quite a valuable collection. Of course, I let a lot of them go, but I don't have to anymore — that's the thing. If I like one, I can just keep it till I die. Then you can have it, and do what you want to with it."

"Do you have to talk like that?"

"Why not?" she said. "I'm not afraid of death. I've had a good life, I've been surrounded by beautiful art that I love. And you're good, too. You are. It's just — "

"What?" I said.

She shrugged. "I had hoped for so much for you, that's all. You could have such a rich life, Blake. I had really hoped to — look, I know this will make you flinch, but I'd really hoped to begin training you to take over here. And now I know that was a mistake."

"Why?"

"Why? Oh, this infatuation with Jon — or *real love,* Blake, that's what you'd like me to call it, isn't it? And your attraction to that whole business . . . the narplehead parents, the just-folks routine . . ."

"I don't know what you're talking about."

"Yes, you do." She picked a cigarette from a packet, lit it, and coolly looked at me. "Oh, yes you do, madam. I reared you to meet world-class artists — as their equal. You've done that already, years before any of your friends could even dream of such a thing. So what do you decide you want? To be married to some Florida beachboy. To be vice-president of a P.T.A.!"

"Look, it's not fair of you to peg me that way — *A.* And *B,* even if what you say is true, don't you know there are women in the world who have done both these things? Had families *and* careers?"

102

"It's not the same," my mother said.

"No, it's not! It's much, much better than what you did!"

"I think you'd better leave," my mother said.

"This is crazy! I came here to apologize."

"*Get out.*" Her voice sounded like a stranger's, unlike any tone she had ever used before. Even her face looked different, ugly and tight. "Get out *now.*"

"I'm leaving," I told her. At that moment, I was sorry I had ever come. I found my way out the door, saw Jon half a block away, and ran to him as fast as I could. He seemed puzzled by my haste, but held his arms out and steadied me when I almost fell. Holding tightly to his arm, I walked toward the restaurant parking lot, a good hike away.

"Home?" Jon said.

I shook my head no. "*Your* home," I said. "Your home. Not mine."

14.

IN the following days, I was polite to my mother. I thought about it and decided that that was how I should be — cooperative, even pleasant. I made small talk with her and watched myself with the fascination an audience has for a skilled actress. It was odd to know that I was talented in this way. As angry as I was, I could still play a convincing model daughter.

And my mother bought my act, or seemed to buy it. Her life went on as it always did; nothing seemed to change. She did begin to give me more money, perhaps as a way of apologizing. I briefly thought about telling her I didn't want it. But in the end, my practical nature won out, and I bought records for my stereo and a Shetland sweater from the People's Republic of China. She complimented the sweater and asked me to turn down the records, please, she was working. Then she pulled out her pocketbook and shamefacedly

— how could she yell at the daughter she really, despite everything, loved? — gave me more.

About this time, she began making phone calls to New York. I did not eavesdrop exactly, but I did overhear enough to know that she was planning another buying trip to Eastern galleries. She planned these trips with the precision of a general plotting a campagn, arranging private viewings at three galleries a day. She never went to more than three, claiming that she would get tired and make bad judgements. And she never went to fewer, saying that the long trip back to the East was expensive and she hadn't gotten rich by not getting her money's worth.

"I need oils," I heard her saying to someone on the phone. "Big, dramatic oils that will dominate a wall. One of my regular clients is building a new solar adobe home and wants great, big oil paintings in blues or greens. Do you have anything like that that's not — how would you say? — too obvious-looking?" Silence. Then, "I don't want to see *one thing* by Matilda Hubert. Matilda Hubert paints garbage! Matilda Hubert's stuff looks like it came from a paint-by-number kit! All right, then. A Maxwell Jenkins is all right. He has talent, you know? Some, anyway."

I drew closer to her. She was rubbing her eyes as if she were tired, too tired to do one more thing. It had been a bad day for her. The maid hadn't come because her brother-in-law was in jail on a bad check charge, and dishes were stacked in the sink. Our kitchen geraniums were dying; the garbage can was full. And I was acting cool to her — polite, as I said, but cool. A refrigerator would have been better company.

"Look, I'll be in on the twenty-eighth around two P.M.," my mother said. "It may be later than two. It won't be earlier, because I'm going to be hitting the West Fifty-seventh Street Gallery at eleven. No, don't send for lunch. Please! No lunch! I know I used to eat like a truck driver, but that was back when I could. The older you get, the harder it is to stay thin."

She hung up the telephone and put her head on her arms. I realized she did not know I was there.

"When are you leaving?" I asked.

She started. Then, in a muffled voice, she said, "Two weeks. Two weeks and a half, to be exact."

"Are you going to be gone long?"

"Not long. Short."

She raised her head and looked at me as if she were trying to decide whether to say something further. Finally she did.

"You want to go with me, Blake?"

"To New York?"

"Sure! You haven't been there in a long time, you know. We could do the galleries together, try some restaurants. Maxie Baehr is going to save me some time. Remember her? What fun she was?"

"She was a lot of fun," I agreed uncertainly. Maxie Baehr was just a big, laughing blur to me.

"You don't have to decide right now," my mother said.

"I'd miss some school."

"You could make it up."

"I'd miss Jon, too."

"You could write postcards to him."

"Well . . ."

"I'm not trying to talk you into anything," my mother said. "It's going to be mostly a working trip. But we haven't been anywhere together in a long time, you know."

"I'd like to go," I said. "But I want to call Jon first."

"Why should you let that boy make your decision for you?"

"I was just going to see if he'd water our plants," I said.

She made an odd sound when she realized what she'd done. "I'm really getting bad, aren't I?" she said.

"Terrible."

"Then I'm sorry."

"No, don't be. It's okay," I promised her. "You're getting middle-aged. Your only kid is getting ready to leave the nest. That's bound to make you nervous, if you think about it."

Her mouth twisted with repressed laughter.

"Anyway, I forgive you," I told her.

At that, she finally broke down and laughed. "Thank you, mother," she said. She whispered, "*Middle-aged! Nervous!*" Then she forgot all about me and went back to the phone.

Jon said yes, of course, he would water the plants, and did I want to go for a ride? When he came to pick me up, he was wearing L.L. Bean corduroys and a Blue Rock sweater. He had begun to look more like a mountain person and less like a Florida import. I approved of the change, at the same time feeling that it made him slightly less exotic. It didn't matter one way or the other, though. John had never had a tacky day in his life.

"You want to go the plaza?" he said, after waving to my phone-talking mother.

"Someplace quieter than the plaza, I think. Where we can talk."

"Where?"

We both thought for awhile, then Jon snapped his fingers. "I know," he said. "Come on."

He left our street and headed for the Camino del Monte Sol, past the Carmelite Monastery and St. John's College, where we saw students sitting around outside, reading before their evening seminars. Foothills studded the landscape, poking into the sky like earthen elbows, erupting with a cover of piñon trees and baby pines and flowering cactus plants. Rabbits, *conejos* the natives called them, flashed here and there behind stunted trees. I followed a fast one with my eyes as it streaked up a steep incline, plunging finally into the bowels of a hill, where it disappeared.

"Where are we going?" I asked.

He was already gliding the car to a halt. "Here."

It was just a turnaround on a dirt road, not particularly private — anyone could see us as they passed — but higher than the cutoffs we had seen before. St. John's spread before us in miniature, its students like ants. For miles around, mountains sprang: the Sangre de Cristos, the Jemez and Sandia. The Albuquerque highway winked from the south like glinting diamonds, as cars began to turn on their lights against the encroaching night.

"Do you like it?" Jon asked softly.

I stared, amazed. "I love it. In all my years in Santa Fe, I don't think I've driven up here."

"I found it a few days ago," he said. "I was saving it for a special occasion. I guess launching you off to New York is special enough."

"I'm not sure I want to go."

"I'm not sure I want you to."

"It'll only be for a few days, you know."

His face grew pensive. "Still."

We were quiet that way for a long time, listening to the wind blow through the skeletal arms of chamisa plants. I thought about New York, my mother, the difficulties of the preceding weeks. I was so knotted in thought that I was barely aware of Jon's arm slipping around me, Jon's hand finding my hand and tightening around it.

"I love you," I thought I heard him say. But it could have been the wind, it was said so softly. I stiffened, wondering if my imagination had been working against me, when he said it again in a surer voice. "I love you, Blake. I do."

I wanted to respond, but my throat closed.

"Have you never said it to anyone?" he asked.

"Never."

"Why not?"

"Too young," I said. "And I'm not sure it's such a good thing, anyway."

"How do you mean?"

"I was thinking about my father and mother," I admitted. "They were in love. A lot of good it did them."

"Think of mine, then," Jon said. "They're still in love. It doesn't happen as often as it used to.

But it does happen once in awhile. It could happen, I guess, to us."

"How do you know when something like that happens?"

"You don't, all at once. I guess it grows on you."

"You mean you've been thinking about this for a long time?" I asked.

"Yes."

"And this place? You drove me here for this, so you could tell me?"

"On top of a mountain," he agreed sheepishly. "It's dumb, I know. But you'd have to grow up where there were no mountains, to appreciate a sight like this one. Look, you're obviously not going to say anything back to me, now." He put the key into his ignition, turned it. "We might as well go home."

"Wait! Can you wait?"

He turned to look at me.

"I can tell you that I feel the same way you do," I said. "But it's hard to say. I feel it but I can't say it."

"Ever?"

"Yet. All I meant was, I can't say it yet."

"But you do feel it?"

"Intensely."

At that, we both began to laugh. It was funny, after all, my inability to put into words what I had been thinking about for weeks.

"So when do you think you can say this — thing?" Jon demanded.

"Summer, maybe. This is spring, right? It'll take a few weeks. Give me till then."

111

"June?"

"July. Maybe even August, if you give me a hard time." But even as that came from my mouth, I knew it was a lie. I loved Jon Purcell as much as the mountains that spread on all sides of us, and I loved them as much as I could love anyone, anything.

"Don't be long," Jon said, "in New York."

"I won't."

"Bueno," he told me. Without knowing it, he had slipped into the vernacular of Santa Fe for the first time since I had seen him with his parents on the plaza, months and a jumbled innocence ago.

15.

IT should have come as no surprise that my mother, so invincible in all other ways, was a paradigm of courage on our flight back East.

No one worries about airplane rides anymore. I don't, anyway, and yet ten minutes before we were to land at Kennedy International, our nervous-sounding captain came on the intercom and said that we had a flat tire. The whole left side could be flat, he said. Then he repeated himself — *could* — to minimize the danger.

We were not to be alarmed if we saw fire trucks and police cars on the landing strip. They weren't in the way. They were there waiting for us, in case we "needed" them.

My mother, who is not religious, listened to the captain's spiel and quietly watched a little old lady on the other side of the aisle do her rosary. Then she ordered a drink from the stewardess and whipped out a *People* magazine, as if everything were perfectly normal. When the big jet finally lurched onto the ground, with flashing fire trucks and screaming ambulances circling unnecessarily around it, she was copying a recipe from "Diets of the Movie Stars." I felt as if my liver was making a quick exit by way of my mouth.

"I didn't know John Travolta would eat chicken. Did you?" she said. "Thought the man was a vegetarian."

"We're not dead," I informed her.

She folded her *People* and stuck it into a leather briefcase, along with checkbooks and a pile of art catalogues. "You weren't really concerned, were you?"

I was too busy trying not to throw up to give her a quick reply.

"I always say, never be too concerned. Look, there's Maxie waving at us! I can't believe she came here to fetch us. Thought she'd send a car, but never this. . . ."

All around us, passengers with sagging knees and trembling fingers gave way to my mother, who touched up her lipstick, freshened her cologne, then hoisted her briefcase like a flag and barged out the door. Watching her, I wondered if she had had even one one bad minute. I doubted it.

"Blake!" she called back into the cabin. "Do you want to be left? Come on!" She pushed into the crowd like a spaniel going after water ducks, her sunglasses winking against the big city's smog. After Santa Fe, the air in New York seemed thick and viscous. I breathed with difficulty, half-faint when I finally shook Maxie Baehr's hand.

My mother's old friend was amazing-looking.

She was squat and energetic, wrapped in a dress that was halfway between russet and red. Her hair was clipped and silver, her hands heavily ringed. She spoke with a slight wheeze that indicated city air wasn't much better for her than it was for me, and her flushed peasant face contrasted sharply with the expensive quality of her clothes. It struck me that the art world had been as good to her as it had been to my mother — maybe better. The car we stepped into was a fine limousine.

"Oh, Lois, doesn't she look like him?" Maxie breathed, once we were all settled in the back seat, watching the New York traffic whiz by.

I was curious. "Him?"

"Your father. You look extraordinarily like him. Surely your mother's told you before?"

"It's nothing I dwell on," my mother said.

"But isn't it incredible?"

"Incredible," my mother dryly agreed. With a politician's sense of conversation, she changed the subject to her need for new oils.

We passed the place on Tenth Street where my mother had had her first gallery, not far from the old Tenth Street School of Painting. It was a European Chocolate Shop now; the new tenants made chocolates by hand, Italian-style, and sold them for a lot of money.

"It still has such good light," my mother said to Maxie as the signals changed and the driver lurched ahead. "I'll never forget the weeks and weeks I spent hunting for light like that at a price I could afford to pay. Then we put in spotlights, of course. But not many. Just a few. There was

115

this great goldeny feeling about that front room — the one they're using for a sales room now. It was incandescent, don't you think, Maxie? Like a Vermeer."

"Did you ever take me to work with you?" I asked.

"Yes."

"Was I a bad baby? Did I get in the way?"

"Yes." But she was smiling, as if my bothering her at work had been just fine. Maybe it had. Or maybe it had been horrible for her, and the years had somehow erased all that.

Maxie's big apartment looked out onto Central Park, which was congested with people: joggers and bicycle riders, mothers pushing babies in prams. She had very little furniture, which was somehow a surprise, and lavish, expensive artwork all over her walls, which was no surprise at all. I almost bumped into a Picasso etching.

"Real?" I asked.

Maxie grinned, not at all offended. "Real. There's another just opposite — see? They're not his best, but they're authentic."

"Maxie's had those for years and years," my mother said. "Picked them up cheap. I used to try to deal for them, but she'd never listen."

"Still wouldn't," Maxie said cheerfully. "I'd give up anything before I'd give up those."

"You practically did. Remember how poor we all were? It was funny, Blake. We used to sit under honest-to-goodness Picassos, museum pieces really, and eat beans and rice, because it was all we could afford. All the money went for art, every penny."

"Unless someone made a big sale," Maxie remembered. "Then we ate like kings. Remember? Whoever made the big commission cooked for everyone else. What days those were!"

"They weren't always easy, though," my mother said.

"No," Maxie agreed. "You're right. They weren't."

I had the uncomfortable feeling then that I was intruding on something that had nothing to do with me. It was like eavesdropping in a restaurant, or accidentally watching someone undress through a window. The moment passed, and I rejoined the conversation.

But for a while there, I had a sense of my mother as a stranger — someone completely unknown to me.

It was a feeling I expected to leave, but as the days in New York passed, it strengthened.

We went into galleries, and business stopped, everything stopped, so the salespeople and artists could meet Lois Strong. Strangers pulled her away from the buying tables to quiz her about her work. Did she really know Georgia O'Keeffe; had she really been to O'Keeffe's home in Abiqui? Had she actually built her famous collection from half a dozen oils?

My mother answered their questions, introduced me, then returned to her work. When she did, they pumped me. How did it feel to be Lois Strong's daughter? Was it wonderful?

Wonderful, I said, but that's not what I thought. *You should try to be the daughter of an art world star. It's awful sometimes. I don't want to be her shadow!*

Our next-to-the-last night in the city, Maxie Baehr threw an enormous party. Two hundred people came, about a fourth of them were faces I recognized from magazines. They wore glitter and plunging necklines, and they knew just how to pose when newspaper photographers came their way.

My mother wore a simple white dress that night, and no jewelry at all. She was tan from walking outdoors in Santa Fe, but had no other color in her face. I think she was the most beautiful woman there, but I cannot tell you why. There were faces younger, more artfully designed, and it would be years before I would realize that what was missing in those faces, and something my mother had in abundance, was character, which throws off a glow of its own.

The party went on and on, with my mother kissing old friends and exclaiming as someone she hadn't seen in years would come through the door. It was odd, but the people she had known when they were all poor and struggling, were now prosperous, the backbone of the art world. And they loved my mother. I watched their expressions carefully, and to a person, what I saw was respect and love.

It made my insides twist to think of the differences in how the world perceived my mother, and how I had always seen her myself. For the rest of the night, until the last guest went home, I sat in the corner and watched the famous, distinguished woman, who had changed my diapers and registered me in kindergarten and pulled strings to get me into Brendan Art Camp, move around the room to greet her friends. Her public.

When it was over, she went straight to bed. It had been tiring, all those memories marching up and saluting. That left Maxie and me and a big mess.

"Don't worry," Maxie said when I began picking up cocktail napkins. "The maid will get it in the morning. You can rest."

I sat down, rubbed my eyes.

Maxie lit a cigarette and surveyed the clutter with a faint smile. "Did you think it was a good party?"

"Yes. A great one."

"You should have seen the parties your mother and I threw when we were younger," Maxie said. "They cost a fraction of this, and in some ways they were a lot more fun."

"Tell me about that," I urged.

"About what?"

"About those days. My mother talks a lot about them, but she doesn't tell me — "

"What?"

"Much of anything personal," I finished, hitting on a truth that had escaped me before. "She never mentions my father, just art. I wonder about that a lot. It's as if he didn't even matter to her."

"Oh, he mattered," Maxie said.

"Can you tell me about it?"

She sighed, mashed her cigarette, and lit another. In some ways, her eyes were like sad clown

119

eyes. Even when she smiled, and she practically always smiled, there was a hint of melancholy there.

"It doesn't surprise me that Lois can't talk about it," she said. "You have to understand your mother. Well, you do, I'm sure. That was a presumptious thing to say. It's only — "

I leaned forward, staring past Maxie to the dying lights of the park.

"Your mother was very young when she met your father," she began abruptly. "Barely into her twenties. She was a very beautiful woman. People used to stop and stare at her, she was so beautiful. Thought she was a model or an actress. But Lois hardly noticed. All she thought about was art."

"That hasn't changed," I said.

"No? Well." Maxie pulled at a bracelet as if she could call up memories that way. "Anyway, she met your father — at one of my parties, I think — and fell in love with him. She'd been married before, you know, a very short marriage, and wasn't wanting to 'get mixed up with a man' — that's how she put it. But there was Peter Cannaberry, who was every bit as handsome as she was beautiful. *And* he'd just come in from England and was as lonely as your mother. So they began to date. It was a bad idea. I told her so and lots of other people told her so. But she wouldn't listen. Said she was in love. And I guess that she was. Peter was, I know."

"Why was it a bad idea?"

"Because they were such completely different people! What your mother loved, Peter hated.

And vice versa. They used to get into these won-
derful fights. Do you remember the old Tracy-
Hepburn movies? They'd get into fights like that.
Your mother would do the Katherine Hepburn
part of the fight and your father would be Spencer
Tracy. They fought about everything! But do you
know, despite that, it was one of the deepest loves
I think I've ever seen."

"What happened?"

"Oh, they married. You know that. That was in
the days when women married and stayed home.
Can you imagine your mother being a housewife?
She worked very hard at it, scrubbing and baking
from scratch and keeping you in starched dresses.
Everything had to be perfect for Peter. She told
everyone she was very happy, but the truth was,
she was miserable. Your father had his work,
which was beginning to take off, and your mother
had her housekeeping. I truly think that marriage
might have made it if she'd said, 'Look, Peter,
I'm working, too.' But the way things were, you
see, that relationship was her whole life. And it
was simply never perfect, Blake. They had
strongly conflicting personalities. After awhile,
they quit fighting for fun and started fighting for
real. And then one day, your mother was at my
apartment. And she was crying, and you were
crying, and Peter had gone back to England.
There was no nasty final scene, he'd just been offered a job there. He'd taken it, and he'd 'forgotten the two of you.'"

I tried to imagine my mother crying over a man,
but I couldn't do it. I could easily imagine her

121

crying when Maxie Baehr had refused to sell her Picasso etchings, but this other thing sounded like a fairy tale.

I must have looked doubtful, because Maxie said, "Oh, it's true. Every word. Your mother almost had a nervous breakdown then. She lost a ton of weight, and she was one of those women who really didn't have it to lose. And then, there was the time when she realized that she was flat broke. She couldn't get a job — all the jobs required traveling, and she couldn't travel with you. You had asthma and allergies, I seem to remember. Plus, the cost of a sitter or a nurse would have been too much. That was when she started trading her pictures. She did incredibly well, almost by accident, really. Then she lucked into a part-time job at a gallery, where she made connections with artists and made other trades. All of a sudden she had money! Then she started her own gallery, and you know the rest. She used to take you everywhere in those days. I honestly think she would have died, if it hadn't been for you. She used to talk to you as if you were an adult. You'd sit in your baby carry-all, and she'd talk finances with you. It was a game. Oh, she talked about everything with you. She rarely let you out of her sight. You were like a pet to the artists. She wanted you to be a happy child and know that you were loved, perhaps because she didn't feel loved herself." She took a pull of her cigarette and looked at me coolly. "I've often wondered if that worked. So tell me, *are* you happier than she?"

Out on the streets, a car careened wildly. Everything else was silent.

"I want to be," I said. Maxie looked at me as if she were thinking: *Go on.* So words tumbled from my mouth. I found myself telling her all about Santa Fe, Jon, the Purcells. I told her, too, about my mother's odd resentment of them.

"He finally told me he loved me," I said.

"Do you love him?"

"I think I do. But I couldn't tell him that."

"Why?"

"Perhaps because my mother wouldn't have approved?" I guessed. Then, "Oh, that's too easy. I don't know. That's the truth, Maxie. I just don't know."

"I think you have to leave your mother out of this," Maxie said. "I have very particular reasons for saying that."

"Well?"

"What you have to remember," Maxie told me then, "is that your mother had wanted a life like the Purcells' very, very much. She *loved* your father, Blake! You didn't come from a marriage of convenience. I wonder if, when she sees you and Jon, she just doesn't worry about your getting hurt."

"But the Purcells didn't get hurt!"

"Lots of people don't," Maxie said cheerfully. "And you may not. You're very young, but who's to say that this won't last? The point is, your mother isn't anti-love or anti-marriage. Not at all, so don't try to paint her that way. What she is, I think, is *pro*-caution. I do know that she'd like you to build your own life a bit more, before you settle down and try to share it with anyone else."

"College, you're talking about."

"College. Art Camp. A period of work. That kind of thing."

"And if I still wanted Jon after all that — you don't think she'd mind?"

"I don't think she'd mind," Maxie said. Suddenly she looked very tired. I became aware of the lateness of the hour and apologized for keeping her up.

"Not at all," she told me, but put her hand over her mouth to stifle a yawn. It occurred to me that she and my mother had talked over these things; that that was the reason she'd known what to say.

Maxie began turning off lights, blowing out candles. I thanked her and went to bed myself, but before I did, I went into my mother's room. She was sleeping at an odd angle, with covers thrown off, and I straightened them before I left.

"Good night," she muttered through a haze of sleep.

I bent down to kiss her, full of Maxie's stories and impressions of the evening. Her hand knotted and unknotted on the pillow as a bad dream passed.

"Good night," I said.

16.

WHEN we returned to Santa Fe, a freakish spring snow blanketed the Sangres. People walked around in insulated vests and bare arms, wearing dazed expressions. It was baseball season after all, and three inches of white covered the ground.

Jon was cross-country skiing when I phoned. It would probably be the last snow of the year, his mother apologized. I hadn't called from New York, so he didn't know what time I would return. Could he call me back?

"Don't frown," my mother said when I hung up. "You always look like a gorilla when you frown."

"I thought he'd be home, that's all."

"He'll come see you as soon as he gets in."

"I guess."

"We could go to the gallery," she said, "and

125

plan where to hang some of the new pictures. Would you like that?"

I know I would not like that at all, but I went to my closet and dug in the back for a winterized parka just the same. By the time I had it on, my mother was already pushing out the door.

We worked for an hour in her storeroom, making space for the new oils that were to be shipped. Bad things had happened in the gallery since my mother left. The posting wasn't done on time, and her gross receipts tax was late. Tax officials had written to my mother, asking for their money and fining her five dollars. Upset, she made a fifteen-dollar phone call to Albuquerque, yelling at her accountants about the slip-up. I sat in a corner of the room and watched her, fascinated. She was completely happy. Crises, instead of wearing her down, gave her an attractive glow.

"Are you hungry?" she asked after slamming down the receiver with a satisfied *thunk*.

"I could eat something."

"I'm very hungry. How would you feel about eating Coquilles St. Jacques?"

Coquilles St. Jacques is my favorite dinner in the world, practically. "What's the special occasion?"

"Just coming home," my mother said. "Tell the secretaries where we'll be, won't you, Blake? Tell them to close up in an hour. After dinner we can walk on home. Go on — I have to make one more call."

When she came out, we hiked the short way to Canyon Road, the Arts and Crafts road of Santa Fe, our boots crunching tracks into the crusted-over snow. All the shops and restaurants were burning piñon wood in their Indian fireplaces; the smell hung in the air like incense. The sun cast a mauve light on the Sangres as we walked past the adobe walls and coyote fences. When we reached Le Mirage, the restaurant my mother had selected, the tables were already candlelit. The place was beginning to get busy, with waiters frantically setting out crystal and silver. There was a line for service, but when the headwaiter spotted my mother, he pushed her ahead of the others, asked about our trip to New York, and automatically brought her her favorite hors d'oeuvres, a platter of garlic-and-butter snails. She was curling a fat one out of its shell with a small silver fork, when our waiter came forward and whispered in her ear.

"It's all right," she said, blotting her lips with a napkin. "He's invited. Bring him over, would you, please?"

I shot her a questioning look, then turned my eyes to the door. Following the waiter was a six-foot boy, who stood out like a sore thumb from the rest of the diners. His face was bright red from a day of skiing, and he still wore his goggles pushed back into his hair.

"Jon?" I said, not believing my eyes. "*Mother?* Did you invite him?"

She polished off the last of her snails and made a deprecating gesture. "You're no fun when you're miserable," she said. "So I asked myself what would make you *less* miserable. And it came to me — "

I lost the rest of the sentence. Almost knocking

my chair to the floor, I ran to meet him, grabbing his chapped hands with my warm ones, and pulling him back to our corner of the room.

Shortly after dessert, my mother excused herself, saying she wanted one more look at her inventory, and would we like to go on home without her? She promised she would not be long.

"You said you wanted to go straight home," I reminded her.

"I changed my mind. There's something I need to check."

"Do you want us to walk back with you?"

"Not particularly," she said, looking at me as if I were an idiot. "I thought you and Jon might have some catching up to do, without an old lady hanging on to your every word."

After another token protest or two, we took off in opposite directions.

"Why did you want her to come with us?" Jon demanded.

"I didn't."

"But you said!"

"I just wasn't sure it would look good, my wanting to be alone with you as badly as that," I admitted. "That would have embarrassed me. I'm not sure exactly why."

"There's nothing wrong with your wanting to be alone with me," he said.

"No."

"In fact, all I thought about while you were gone was being alone with you," Jon told me. "I had lots of fantasies about that. My mother told me I was sitting around with a dumb look on my face, to go out and get some fresh air. So I did. That's why I was gone when you called today."

"Skiing?"

"Right. It was to get some fresh air and get the dumb look off my face. That's a direct quote, if you couldn't already tell."

I laughed, but his words had an odd effect on me. By the time we spotted my house, its darkness looked almost menacing. I hesitated when we reached the door.

"Do you want to come in?" I said.

"Of course. I'll come in and we'll wait around for your mother. What time do you think she'll be home?"

"I don't know," I admitted.

Jon shrugged. "That's all right. My parents know where I am. They know better than to worry about me. Sure, I'll come in."

"It's hard to see, I can't tell which . . ."

"Here." He pulled the key ring away from me, fumbled until he found the right key, and inserted it neatly into the lock. With a practiced twist, he let us in.

There was a small brass lamp burning in the room, and Jon pushed my hand down when I tried to turn on the overhead light.

"One's enough," he said. "Don't you think?"

I tried to say something, but his mouth was on mine before I could make a sound. Somehow he maneuvered me to my mother's couch, or we maneuvered each other; I have to be honest about how that came about. He kissed me harder and longer than he ever had, and a general weakening overcame me, a lack of desire to stop the kissing and start up something else — a conversation, a walk.

Suddenly I felt a sense of alarm — not danger exactly, but a knowledge that if I did not pull back then, I could not pull back at all. Ideas I had had about men and women stopped being vague and became very, very clear. I intuitively knew what the next steps would be and what that would mean.

"Get up!" The sound of my voice shocked me; I had not meant to say anything at all.

"You don't want me to," Jon said, clinging to me. "You don't really want me to stop now. You don't . . ."

But I was already off the couch. Trembling. Cold.

Jon was unable to look at me, or talk to me.

"I'm sorry," I said — less because I was, than because I couldn't imagine what else to say.

"I couldn't wait for you to get back; I couldn't wait to hold you," he muttered. "I thought you felt the same."

He bolted from the room. The front door clicked shut. I wandered to the front window and tried to follow him with my eyes, but he was already gone.

"I'm sorry," I said again, this time to the dark street. Then I began to cry. I had not really wanted to fight my way out of that, but I knew that it wasn't yet time. And I also knew that if Jon had asked me, I could not even tell him why.

"I knew better than to leave you like that," my mother swore.

I had not told her what happened with Jon. I didn't have to. She had passed him as he ran blindly across East Palace Street. Then she had walked into the darkened living room and looked at my face. And she had known.

"It's not your fault."

"Whose fault is it, then? You *asked* me to go home with the two of you! But I thought you were just being polite."

"I was."

"I should have come with you anyway. The truth is, my brain was turned off. I'm sorry."

"It's all right."

"No, it's not." She huddled into the couch, shaking her head. "You know, it's very hard to be a mother these days. I could have predicted this, but then you would have told me I had a dirty mind. On the other hand, by pretending that you and Jon were still in kindergarten, that there was no physical attraction at all, I feel responsible for your having had a very bad time."

I stared at her out of the corner of my eye. "You don't want me to see him again, do you?"

"I can't keep you from seeing anyone. You know that."

"But you don't want me to see him. Do you?"

"Blake." She reached for a cigarette and lit up. "What I want for you is happiness. And I want you never to be hurt. Now, one of those is a possible thing, and the other isn't. And even though I'm older than you, and even though I'm your mother" — here she broke into theatrical shudders — "I'm smart enough to know which is which."

131

"Are you saying I *should* see him?"

"Well, you missed him enough in New York, didn't you? He's the great love of your life so far, isn't he?"

"So far he is," I said.

"Well, then."

A look much like pain crossed my mother's face. Then, incongruously, she laughed. "I can't believe we're having this conversation," she said. "I could never have talked with my own mother about love and sex. She would have killed me! And she would have been full of judgments, too. Rules were very clear, back then. If you let your boyfriend touch you, you were bad. If you didn't, you were good. Everyone was worried about pregnancy and reputations."

"They still are."

"But a lot of them grow up faster than we did."

"That's true," I said.

"I'm not sure if I'm the one to advise you about this," she told me. "I still feel a lot of the old ways were right. There's something to be said for waiting, you know."

"I know," I told her.

She looked doubtful and embarrassed. It was one of the few times in my life I had ever seen my mother less than poised.

"That's why I did what I did," I said.

Mother looked away.

"But I do like him better than anybody. I think if I promised you I wouldn't see him again — that would be a promise I couldn't keep."

"Then don't make it," she told me.

"I don't think I will."

132

She got up from the couch and moved toward her room. I watched her, wondering what had happened with her when she had been in love with my father. She must have read my mind, for she stopped midway to her room and smiled. "I don't think I'm ready to go through this with you."

"Good night," I said.

"Good night. If you need to talk about this more, do you promise to let me know?"

"I need to talk about it more," I said. "But the one I need to talk about it with, I think, is Jon."

EPILOGUE

THE snow was almost gone when I awoke the
following day. It had been an oddly warm
night for mountain altitude, and our yard jutted
baldly where Jon's footsteps had been frozen just
hours before. What little snow was left branched
out from shady corners like ghostly limbs of trees.
I looked for my mother and discovered that she
had already gone to the gallery. So I dressed and
went out for a walk alone, hoping that the combination of sun and fresh air would help me forget
the night before.

The weather had almost worked its medicine
when I arrived back home and found Jon waiting
on the front porch.

"I wasn't going to see you today," he said. "But
I thought I'd better. I thought if I didn't, we'd
never get together again."

I stood where I was and watched him, uncertain
of what to say.

"I can't help feeling the way I do, but I shouldn't have done what I did," he said.

"What did you do?"

"I sort of attacked you, didn't I? You must think I'm a maniac today."

"We sort of attacked each other, Jon," I muttered. "That was the frigtehning thing. Anyway, 'attacked' is a lousy word to use. Nothing violent happened. Everything was great. That's what scared me most of all."

"Do you think we'd better stop seeing each other for a while?"

"No."

"Good," he said, relief flooding his face. "Because I don't know what would happen to me if I couldn't see you anymore."

"You'd be fine," I told him. "Nothing would happen to you at all." I wasn't trying to be hard or cold, but it occurred to me that whatever happened between us, we'd still be apart for awhile. In the hours between his leavetaking and our seeing each other again, I'd decided I had to get away to think about what was happening to us, and to me. I had taken out my brochure on Brendan Art Camp and had studied it until I'd fallen asleep. And when I woke up, I had simply and suddenly felt good about going there. It was one of those times when I'd wondered and wondered about right things to do. And then I quit wondering. Everything seemed quite clear.

The days ahead were both easy and hard. Sometimes going away seemed the best idea I'd ever had. Other times, I would think of Jon with other girls (more grown-up, more accommodating girls) and knot up from the pain of leaving him, though I realized I might not lose him at all.

At those times, everything good I felt for Jon came welling up, tightening my chest until I felt I would explode. I needed both to be with him, and to be away.

Loving someone and staying with him seemed like such a simple thing to me, almost a given.

And yet it was so hard.

My mother and father had been unable to carry it off. Now Jon and I were having shaky days.

I tried to think why that was so. It seemed that we had less a problem of love than a problem of balance.

Jon was a powerful force in my life, as powerful as my mother had always been before. I wondered if it were possible for two bright stars to burn in tandem, instead of one eclipsing the other at every turn. Jon and my mother were both suns, and when I deferred to one of them, I became a shadow.

And that was a role I no longer wanted to play.

This is when people quit trying, I realized. Then another thought came: *No one says you have to be like them.*

Because I knew I still wanted to work things out, even if it meant throwing out all the old answers that had failed and scrambling for new ones myself. There had to be a better way to love than my mother had found — or even the Purcells. Perhaps it was possible to take the best from my family, and the best from Jon's, and meld them until they were one.

I surveyed the house I was about to leave —
the window where I watched the cardinals feed,
the pueblo fireplace with its flickering piñon logs,
the wonderful art that hung on the walls. Then I
looked outside and saw Jon walking up in his tar-
tan plaid jacket, a serious expression on his face.

Let everything be all right, I wished.

As if he could hear me, the tension on Jon's
face lessened. He saw me in the window and made
a jaunty half-wave. Rain began falling, the hard,
thundering kind that pelts the junipers, weighing
down their boughs. A drop caught him in the eye,
then another, and he swiped at them, laughing.

Then he hurried up the drive, dodging puddles
and potholes, and made his way through the open
door.